Flightfall

ALSO BY ANDY STRAKA
Frank Pavlicek Mysteries:
A Witness Above • A Killing Sky • Cold Quarry
The Night Falconer
A Witness Above *(Teen Edition with Falconry Primer)*
Suspense:
Record of Wrongs
The Blue Hallelujah

Praise for the Pavlicek series:

One of "Ten Rising Stars in Crime Fiction."
—*Publishers Weekly*

"A great read."
—*Library Journal*

"Fast-paced, twisty, and complex."
—Booklist

"A book this good, and this original, helps remind me why I
started reading mysteries in the first place."
—Steve Hamilton

A Frank Pavlicek Mystery

Flightfall

by Andy Straka

Cedar Creek Publishing
Virginia, USA

Library of Congress Control Number 2013935063

978-0-9891465-2-4

Cedar Creek Publishing
Virginia, USA
www.cedarcreekauthors.com

"How do the birds make great sky circles . . .
They fall and falling they are given wings."
—Jalal Rumi

1

The day Jake Toronto triggered the downfall of a cable TV network, I was in my office thinking about my upcoming vacation. My suitcase, already packed for the beach, sat in the corner. An image of my wife Marcia in her bikini floated in and out of my mind. Nicole worked on her computer in the office next to mine. I was busy tending to some last minute paperwork that included shuffling through a stack of soon-to-be-due bills at the moment to determine who, beside myself, was most in need of getting paid.

Toronto's text pinged my mobile. I barely noticed and didn't even bother giving it a look. The fax went off at the same time, the one down the hall we shared with the web startup and the two Russians, and I almost ignored it, too. The machine was probably spitting out another cryptic cipher bearing specs for Slavic network servers like those the two Russians occasionally received. Then again, it could be a missive from one of our lawyer clients informing us we'd been named in some multi-million dollar lawsuit.

"Did you hear the fax?" I asked loudly enough to be heard through my open door.

"What?" Typing away on her keyboard, Nicole had apparently ignored the sounds as well.

"Never mind. I'll get it."

The first Thursday in a Charlottesville August was a scorcher. Hot enough to spawn insta-sweat for anyone who ventured outside. Through my window, down on Water Street, two men from the phone company worked a bucket truck against a pole. The five o'clock sun threw long shadows from the buildings. Across town, the university slept its summer slumber. Traffic moved as if in a dream. Almost everybody we did business with– attorneys, insurers, and other ne're-do-wells–was away somewhere on vacation. A persistent fly darted around my office, confident, apparently, that he owned the place.

He could have it, as far as I was concerned. Nicole would keep the creaky wheels of commerce–such as they were– running, while I, in a matter of hours, would be joining Marcia on the sand at the Outer Banks with one of her custom made Rum Daiquiris in my hand.

To celebrate, I had taken an extra long lunch on a bench beneath one of the poplars lining the downtown mall in order to finish the final chapters of Mark Helprin's Memoir from Antproof Case. I had even splurged on a new Hawaiian shirt recommended by that impresario of tropical wear Dave Taylor, owner of my favorite Charlottesville bookshop, Read It Again Sam. Might as well try to get started on my vacation a little early.

I was just about to rise from the chair to check out the offending fax when a door opened across the hall. The wall vibrated as someone clomped over to the machine. The building's part-time receptionist had already escaped for the day, but it didn't make any difference: secrets never lasted around here. There was a delay before I heard the sheet being ripped from the platen. Then the clomping continued to my half-open door.

"For you," a voice said.

It belonged to one of the Russians, a curious combination of foreign and acquired Dixie undertones. He stood in the doorway, the curled paper lodged between his meaty fingers. An amiable fellow, big and broad-shouldered. His nose had long ago been surrendered to a roseacea that seemed to ripen further every time I saw him.

"Thank you." I stood and took the sheet from him.

He didn't move.

"Business okay?" I tried not to sound too encouraging of discourse.

"Some days okay . . . Some days, not so okay."

I nodded. He still didn't move.

"Today?" I asked.

"Not so okay." He finally turned and left, his feet falling less loudly down the hall than before.

Returning to my chair, I uncurled the fax. The Russian was right. It was for me and I didn't like what I was reading.

I glanced at my suitcase in the corner, already packed for the beach, and sighed.

"Hey, Nicky," I called through the doorway into the next office. "Any idea why Toronto would be sending us a fax?"

"A fax?"

"Yeah. It sure looks like it's from him."

Her curiosity aroused, the chair squeaked as she pushed away from her screen. "Unless it's a formal document requiring a legal signature, the only reason he might send a fax," she said, "is if he's somewhere out in the woods. Remember he's got that old beat up cell phone and fax gizmo set up in his Jeep."

Most of the time, Toronto stormed around the planet with a healthy amount of the latest high tech gadgetry, communications gear, and weaponry available to man. But not when he was out hunting or flying hawks or falcons. He thought it went against the purity and ancient roots of the art to be armed with anything more.

"He wouldn't be out hunting this time of year," I said. Toronto's falconry birds, like ours, had been put up for the season a couple of months before and, except for training and exercise flights, were eating like kings and molting their feathers in their mews.

"True." Nicole padded around the corner in her sandals and cutoff shorts. Call me biased, but my daughter had developed into quite an attractive young woman. She wore her dark hair shoulder-length. Her eyes curved into delightful ovals and her cheekbones were high as any models. Her skin was nicely tanned and the only flaw in her face, if it could even be called that, was the Pavlicek nose, which was a little wide but otherwise nicely proportioned. "You think he's in some kind of trouble?"

I finally glanced at the text message on my phone. They were the same words as the ones on the fax. "See for yourself." I let out a long breath.

"Looks like he really wants to get in touch with us." She came around the side of my desk as I turned the document toward her.

"COULD REALLY USE YOUR HELP," both the paper and the text message read. "DEATH IN THE FAMILY. . . . JAKE."

2

The buck snorted at our approach, then disappeared, hooves crashing into the pitch-black woods.

Probably curious, and who could blame him? For a moment his great head of antlers had been caught in the glare from the floodlights burning on stanchions out here in the middle of nowhere. The lamps cast an arc of light against the trees overspreading the edge of the clearing and were surrounded by a perimeter of power cords and mark tape, making the location looked like something out of The Blair Witch Project.

From somewhere in his bag of tricks, Toronto had obviously brought in the heavy crime scene artillery. We should have expected as much. My former NYPD partner was nothing if not anal-retentive.

"Sorry again about the timing," he said, as he scrambled off to check on one of his bank of lights that was flickering.

He knew I was headed away on vacation. But he'd also known I would answer his call for help. After he explained to me in more detail on the phone what had happened, I didn't hesitate. Loyalty is loyalty, after all, and Jake Toronto would swim through a river full of anacondas for me or Nicole.

He had specified where and when we should wait for him, leaving my truck to plink and pop to silence behind his battered Jeep on the fire road down the mountain. It had been an eighty mile drive over the Blue Ridge, down 1-81, and across 1-64 into the Allegheny highlands. Not exactly next door. I called Marcia from the truck to explain the situation. She seemed to understand, or at least acted as if she did–that is if anyone could understand the obsession Toronto, Nicole, and I shared.

On the drive over, Nicole and I had talked.

"You think Jake's crazy, Dad?"

"Who, Toronto?" I paused. "Never . . . Crazy like a fox, maybe, always on the edge."

"That's what you like about him, isn't it?"

"Maybe."

"You ever miss the danger?"

"What do you mean?"

"You know–working the streets on the force."

"I don't miss the blood."

"But you and Jake always seem to be falling into these kind of situations."

"What kind of situations?"

"You know what I mean . . . you two must be made for battle or something. No matter where you go, you seem to find yourselves in one."

"Is that why you like hanging around working with your Old Man?"

She smiled. "Maybe."

"I know it can't be the pay."

"You're right. It must be your overwhelming charm."

"Hey, hold on a minute. Marcia knows all about my overwhelming charm."

"Which is why she is still waiting for you at the beach."

We rode on in silence for a moment or two.

"I guess we do get into some dicey situations from time to time, though, don't we?" I said finally.

She nodded. "To put it mildly."

"Let's just hope this isn't one of them."

Toronto, with his Roman nose and close-cropped black hair, finally reappeared from working on the lights. He seemed to materialize like an apparition out of the darkness, and his eyes carried a cold glaze that told you something boiled just beneath the surface with which you would not wish to contend. It had taken twenty minutes of hard hiking to follow him back up the ridge. Another five to reach the spot where we'd surprised the deer.

"So let me get this straight," I said to him. "You were doing balloon training up here with the bird before he took off, and you found the body here in the clearing and had it sent down to a lab in Blacksburg for an autopsy?"

The three-sixteenth's Iroquois nodded. "Good people there at the vet school."

Nicole gazed around the glow of the clearing. "And you wanted Dad and me here because . . . ?"

"You're here 'cause you're the big-picture guy," he said.

Right. My big picture now was that we'd reached a small clearing near the edge of what looked like a narrow plateau. A steamy veil supercharged the air. More tape and cords snaked everywhere, and small wire flags dotted the ground as if they were random daisies. Down the hill at the back of the site, the portable generators made enough racket to drown out the tree frogs.

Toronto had transformed this lonely stretch of mountainside into a formal crime scene. At least we were clear about that. Even though I had no idea where the Commonwealth of Virginia statute stood when it came to private investigators looking into an incident such as this.

"Generators need more gas," Toronto said.

He moved to take care of them, hoisting a couple of five

gallon containers with his thick arms like they were featherweights. He wasn't as lean as he'd been in his detective days, but he was stronger, more efficient.

"You said we're pushing fourteen hours since the kill?"

"Exactly . . . Plus a front's moving down from Ohio. Be a monsoon out here before dawn and there won't be much evidence left to see."

"You got a line on where the shooter stood?"

"Not for sure yet . . . Was hoping you could walk it with me." He finished with the gas.

"What else do you know?"

"Jazzman could have been perched in this maple when they shot him." Without looking, he pointed his thumb up and out toward the barely visible forest canopy overhead. "Then again, from the depth of the impression his body left in the dirt, he hit the ground like a rock. My money says he was in flight, maybe even in a stoop."

"That would've been some shot." I turned and looked at Nicole, who'd remained quiet up until this point. "What do you think?"

She nodded. "I think it's going to be tough piecing it together."

A little more explanation might be in order at this point.

The victim in question was a peregrine falcon. A male called a tiercel, affectionately named Jazzman. He had belonged to Toronto, who trapped him under special permit, raised and trained him from a passage bird to the four-year-old hunting falcon he was. Peregrines were no longer an endangered species. But, like all birds of prey, they still enjoyed special government protection. Whoever shot Jazzman had committed a federal crime.

Since we both left the force years before under less than

honorable circumstances, ex-detective Jake Toronto and I had each gone through a metamorphosis. Toronto's was from streetwise Bronx native to naturalist and homesteader in Texas, then to Idaho, then Nebraska, then here, in western Virginia. Along the way, he had taken up the ancient sport of falconry. It had become his passion. Along the way, he'd infected Nicole and me with the same passion. We all flew birds for hunting, kept and trained them, helped each other out. Losing a bird was almost like losing a child to Toronto, to us as well.

Some people said we were nuts. Just nuts enough to be out here with a full court press of an investigation into the murder of a bird. No doubt Toronto had contacted one of his military or government contacts as well, calling in some chits to obtain cell phone, radar, and even any satellite data or images that might be beneficial.

"Your crime scene analysis is incredible," Nicole said, admiring, as she often did, Toronto's technical savvy. "Did you contact the game warden?"

Toronto nodded. "He's out of town, but we've got a meeting with the Sheriff first thing in the morning."

Lightning flashed against distant clouds. "What kind of weapon you think was used?" I asked.

"The vets'll be able to tell us for sure, but from the wound, I'm pretty sure it was a .22–most likely a rifle. Be pretty hard to hit a bird in flight with a handgun."

"Might've just been a kid out shooting cans. Saw the big bird and he couldn't resist."

"Maybe." But his eyes said he didn't think so.

"We could be talking poachers . . . but they left the body. Doesn't fit." A mosquito dive-bombed my ear. I slapped at it.

Toronto nodded and sniffed the wind. He too had seen the lightning.

"Who owns this land? I remember coming up through here with you last year."

"A client," he said.

"Client, huh?"

How Toronto made his living these days was far from clear. He helped Nicole and me when needed, but that was nowhere near every week. He made some money in the market. He did some overseas work on occasion, sometimes disappearing for days even weeks at a time, leaving another falconer, often one of us, to help babysit his hawks. I knew he kept a stack of business cards in his desktop drawer that said he was a "security and special ops consultant," whatever that meant. He could have afforded a stylish mountain chalet closer to town. But he kept to himself, living like a monk in a house trailer on fifty acres of remote land instead.

"Have you talked to this client about the bird yet?"

"Not yet, but I intend to. Want to get everything I can from the scene here first."

I looked around. "Soil and leaf samples gone to the lab too?"

"Uh-huh."

"Any footprints or tracks?"

"A couple. I made a moulage." He led me to the spot where a circle of flags marked the first print. It still glistened from the fixture he'd used. There was a can of hair spray next to a cardboard box that must have contained the moulage, which was basically a mold of the print.

"Looks like a hiking boot," I said.

He nodded again. "Frye. Not big. Size seven. Not deep either. Our trigger was not a heavyweight."

"That narrows it down to only a couple million or so . . . Was the bird's body intact? I mean, any pieces or parts missing?"

Toronto scratched at the stubble on his face. "If you're

thinking rhino tusks here, forget it. There was that scandal back in the eighties. Operation Falcon. Feds caught a couple guys illegally exporting birds and tried to turn it into a sting op. But those were live birds . . . "

My watch read almost eleven p.m. A lot of sane people were fast asleep in their beds right now. A part of me wished I was there too. For his part, Toronto looked as though he was ready to go at it all night.

"So what now?" I bent down to retie the laces of one of my own boots. Not Frye, army-navy generic. My prints would be larger than the shooter's, deeper too.

"I found another partial track about fifty feet into the woods." He pointed along the ridge.

"Okay," I said. "Why don't we see if we can reverse it? If the shooter used an automatic, maybe we'll get lucky and stumble upon some brass."

Toronto, Nicole, and I made our way out of the light through the brush to the second footprint, also marked with a circle of flags. We began a sweep, walking in parallel about three paces apart. I swept my Coleman lantern back and forth in front of me to offer the broadest light.

We had gone about twenty paces when Toronto said, "Got something."

I crossed the beam of his light. He was examining another partial print, this one a heel, and a broken sapling.

I caught a glint of something metallic in the corner of my eye. "Hold it. I've got something, too. Shine your light with mine over here." I bent down to examine the shiny object as Toronto and Nicole stepped up beside me.

"It's a battery," Nicole said.

"The girl's a natural-born sleuth," Toronto said.

She punched him playfully in the arm.

"Double A. Looks pretty fresh." I said. "So our perp or perps must have dropped their GPS or whatever. Maybe in too much of a hurry to split."

"Maybe left us some nice fingerprints, too." Toronto pulled something from his jacket pocket, reached down, and deftly picked up the object with a pair of tweezers, depositing it in a clean paper bag. But before closing the bag, he shone his flashlight on the battery and peered in at it more closely.

"Something about the battery bothering you?" I asked.

"I don't know." He closed and sealed the bag before turning to look at us. "You know, usually if a falconry bird ever gets killed, they're attacked by an eagle or an owl or some other bigger raptor."

"Right."

"Or even stupid, like flying into a transformer, or some farmer or kid takes a pot shot and brings the bird down."

"What are you saying?"

"I'm saying losing Jazzy . . . this feels different somehow."

"Why's that?"

"J-man was wearing a tail transmitter. I was tracking him, but the bullet damaged the unit he was wearing, and I lost the signal. I heard the shot. I was about a half a mile away. Then it took me quite a while to find the body . . ."

"So what does that have to do with the battery?"

"The battery in this bag is the same kind I use in my receiver—even the same brand."

"But there must be millions of that brand of battery sold." Nicole said.

"You think someone else was tracking your bird?" I asked.

"I'm thinking batteries don't grow in the forest," he said. "That's all."

3

We continued searching in the dark for a couple more hours, but found nothing else of value.

By midnight, we were nursing cups of coffee around the kitchen table in Jake's doublewide, a topographical map of the mountain shoved to one side.

"You know what," Toronto said, as if he'd just remembered something important, "I need to get my stuff out of the jeep and go check out my equipment in the barn."

"I'll go with you," I said.

While Nicole cleaned up in the kitchen, Toronto and I hauled the lights and all the forensic material gathered from the Jeep into the barn. Toronto's barn dwarfed his house. There were three indoor/outdoor mews for his falconry birds, and a large, open floor for storing his tractor and other farm equipment. Another section housed an area for work and forensics gear, and behind an alarmed security fence was a locked doorway that led to his security and surveillance gear and weapons cache. After we'd finished stowing the crime scene evidence, Toronto turned with his falconry bag over his shoulder and headed straight for the anteroom to the mews.

His falconry furniture was well organized, neatly laid out on a broad worktable and hung on a pegboard. Hoods, bells, jesses, and leashes. Extra gloves, leatherworking scissors, punches, and imping kit with an array of neatly stored feathers, saved from the molt for use when needed. A smaller table below a cupboard housed his radio tracking transmitters and receiver. He stopped when he reached this table and laid his bag down. He pulled open the cupboard and sighed. One of the shelves inside was empty.

"What's wrong?"

"My backup receiver is gone."

"You sure you didn't take it out and leave it somewhere?"

"I'm sure." He looked at a piece of paper taped inside the cupboard door. "I haven't inventoried this gear in a while. Last time was a month ago. It's definitely gone."

"You think someone stole it?"

"That's what I'm thinking."

"Why?"

"I don't know."

"You think it has anything to do with the battery and Jazzy being shot?"

"That would be the question, wouldn't it?"

As predicted, a storm system blew in as we were all getting ready for bed. Rain pounded against the roof of Toronto's house trailer and the wind shook the windows. Nicole took the spare bedroom while I sacked out on the living room couch, about as far away from the beachfront condo Marcia and I had rented as I could be. Before turning out the light, Marsh and I talked on the phone for a few minutes.

"So let me make sure I have this straight," she said. "You and Nicky are up there in the mountains with Jake instead of you being here at the beach with me because of Jake's peregrine falcon."

"Dead peregrine falcon," I added.

"I understand. And that's awful. But can't Jake and the authorities up there figure out what happened on their own?"

"If it was just some random poacher or farmer, yes. But we think there may be more to it than that."

"How long will you be there?"

"I'm not sure. It's complicated," I said.

She said she understood before we ended the call, but I knew she wasn't telling the truth. I'd have some repair work to do on my marriage if and when I finally made it to the beach.

Maybe Nicole was right. Whoever shot Jazzman could have been half way to Canada by now, or anywhere in between, and here we were up in these midnight mountains chasing phantoms in the dark. Maybe Toronto and I were too eager to stick our noses in places they didn't belong. Maybe we were itching for a fight.

4

The next morning, Toronto, Nicole, and I piled into Toronto's Jeep and drove into Leonardston, the Affalachia County seat. Toronto had already reported the falcon's shooting to the Virginia Department of Game and Inland Fisheries and to the U.S. Fish and Wildlife Service. Unfortunately, as Toronto had already told us, the game warden for the area was on an extended fishing trip to Alaska, and we had to make do with a promised they'd send someone else within a couple of days. The new county sheriff Webster Davies greeted us in the doorway to his office. A wiry, bespectacled man, whose pasty hair made him look more like an old preacher than a sheriff, he was a friend of Toronto.

"Looks to me like there's nothing either the game warden or my people can do that you and your buddies here haven't thought of already."

"Maybe," Toronto said. "But I've got a feeling this shooting was more than just a spur-of-the moment thing."

"This bird was an endangered species, you say?"

"No. Peregrines used to be endangered. But they're still protected under federal law."

We were standing beside the entrance to the jail wing of the county office building, a structure that didn't looked to have changed much since the days of segregation. But the new law enforcement section next door made it look like someone had cobbled on a hardened, high tech command post to the older building. Its walls, bristled with antennas and satellite dishes for video uplink and high speed internet.

"Too bad your bird wasn't endangered. Media, reporters, and the like are always hot after anyone messing with an endangered animal . . . You could really put the heat on someone. How long you say you been flyin' the thing?"

"Two years."

The sheriff nodded. "How about you, Mr. Pavlicek?" He arched his eyebrows in my direction. "What's your involvement in all this?"

"Just here helping out a friend," I said.

"You ain't even showed me no license."

I produced my driver's license and private investigator's license and he looked them over.

"And your daughter, here?'

"She works with me."

"Huh. And you all fly some of these here birds, too, do you?"

"We do."

Sheriff Davies scratched his chin. "Pee-I business must be getting a little slow these days, great recession and all."

"We manage."

"You don't look like no investigator."

Maybe my yellow flip-flops and Elvis Lives with Me T-shirt were throwing him off. I had figured I'd be headed to the beach by now, and hadn't planned on an extended stay.

"I'm supposed to be on vacation," I said.

He grunted in return, glanced at Toronto, who was decked out in a flak jacket, Tony Lama boots, and mirror sunglasses that could have come straight out of a G. Gordon Liddy catalog, before looking back at me. "You two fellas really ex-homicide?"

"That's right," I said. "A long time ago. But . . . "

"But what?" the sheriff asked.

"Let's just say the NYPD doesn't always welcome us back with open arms."

He grunted again and looked at nothing.

"What about the missing receiver?" Toronto asked.

"You mean that electronic gizmo thing you showed me?"

"Right. I have another one just like it and it's missing."

We had spent an hour that morning rummaging through his barn, which he never locked, looking for the second receiver.

"Jake. You know as well as I do, just 'cause you found some battery out there in the woods don't mean somebody was out to kill your hawk." The sheriff worked his jaw as if he needed to spit. "But I suppose it could be. Had a couple old boys got into a dispute with the high school principal a while back. Kilt the family's dog, and no one's seen 'em since. Likely skipped the state . . . Someone upset with you, Jake? Enough to pull a stunt like that?"

"Maybe." Toronto's voice dropped, betraying nothing.

"Well, you'd best be giving that some more thought. Don't you think?"

Toronto nodded.

The sheriff looked down at his watch. "We'll have the battery checked for prints. I know I owe you, Jake, but I can't do much more than that right now. There's a meeting I'm supposed to be at and I'm already late."

5

Toronto's Jeep bounced through a pothole on the way out of the county office parking lot.

"That guy was prehistoric," Nicole said, meaning the sheriff.

"Oh, yeah?" I gave her the evil eye. "What's that make Jake and me then?"

"Just ancient," she said with a wink. "Maybe with a touch of Neanderthal."

"Neanderthal," Toronto said. "Nice."

"What did the sheriff mean when he said he owed you?" I asked.

Toronto shrugged. "He had a deputy thought he was the next Chuck Norris. Asked if I could maybe do anything about it. So I stepped in and helped straighten the guy out."

Toronto and I had worked together for a long time. 'Straighten the guy out' normally involved intimidation, bodily harm, or worse.

Back to what Nicole had been talking about on the trip out. Maybe trouble, violence, whatever, followed Toronto and me around like a trailing shroud. Maybe it went even deeper than that. Maybe it was some kind of karma from our past lives in New York. I think the Old Testament might have even had something to say about that.

"You've already got somebody in mind for killing your falcon, don't you?" I said.

Toronto nodded.

"Well, as your pro bono investigator, I'd certainly appreciate your sharing that information with me. I'm dropping a hundred and fifty bucks a day on a beach condo I'm failing to enjoying at the moment—not to mention leaving a beautiful woman alone to cool her heels."

"Actually," Toronto said. "I have more than one suspect."

"Beautiful," I said.

"There are two."

"I take it these are two people who have a reason to hate you," Nicole said.

Toronto shrugged. "You might say that."

"They might need to get in line," I said.

Nicole ignored me. "They must hate you enough, Jake," she said. "To want to hurt you."

"Sound about right," he said.

"But you're so tough they know they can't get at you directly. And they might have been tempted to take it out on your falcon."

"Now you're making sense. Did you know your daughter's a genius, Frank?"

"I think they call that displaced emotion," I said.

"Right. Thanks for the dissertation, Mr. Freud."

"Your bird didn't kill somebody's Chihuahua, I hope," Nicole said.

"Hardly. You've been reading too many of those tabloid websites. Anyway, those were wild hawks that did that in California."

"So how long are you going to keep us in suspense?" I asked.

"Okay," Toronto said. "Get your hard hats on." He took the next left and pointed ahead to a wide ribbon of paved road that cut around the opposite side of the mountains from his own place. "We're going to visit a school construction site."

6

The school under construction was in a field a few miles farther along the highway. Level land carried a premium price in Affalachia County, and the government controlled more than its fair share of it. The shell of the building had already been erected. Its skeletal structure resembled a flattened beehive surrounded by heavy equipment and a fleet of private cars and pickups. A couple of big cranes hovered overhead while dozens of workers moved in and out of the building.

"The kid we're looking for is named Gabriel Wylie–goes by Gabe," Toronto said.

"Kid?" I asked.

"Sorry. He's probably about Nicky's age here."

"What's his beef?"

"He's approached me a couple of times about my birds. Seems to think I shouldn't have any. He lives in some kind of commune with a bunch of people who grow organic vegetables and make berry juice for a legitimate business while tending a clandestine crop of marijuana on the side. There aren't a lot of secrets around here if you spend time getting to know people."

"What's he doing working construction?"

"Guess he doesn't mind exploiting the environment when there's a good paycheck involved. I hear he's not a bad carpenter, either."

"But why shoot your falcon?" Nicole asked. "He sounds more like the type who wouldn't want to hurt a bird."

"True. But he's also the type who would sneak in and steal my extra tracking receiver. And I know he keeps a rifle. Maybe he was trying to scare Jazzy into flying off for good. Maybe he didn't mean to shoot him."

I nodded. "Stranger things have happened."

The foreman didn't know Toronto, but judging by the respectful nods in our direction, a number of the workers did. We found Gabriel Wylie helping a short Hispanic man carry a stack of boards. Wylie himself was about five foot eight. He had long brown hair, the lean body of a wrestler, and wary eyes.

"Wylie."

The young man turned at the sound of Toronto's voice. "What're you doing here, Toronto?"

"Wonder if we could speak with you for a minute."

His eyes bounced back and forth between Toronto, Nicole, and me. "What's this about?"

"Just want to ask you a couple of questions. That's all."

Wylie turned to his companion and said under his breath in Spanish: "Ahora vengo. Necessito que fumo."

They set down the load of boards and the other man turned and walked away.

"You smoke, too," Toronto said.

"What?" Apparently, Wylie didn't think any of us spoke Spanish.

"Never mind."

"All right, you showed up here with your little entourage, and if you hang around here much longer, you're going to get me in trouble. What do you want?"

"Where were you yesterday?"

"Where was I? I was here working."

"All day?"

"On the job all day. You can ask anybody. Must have been fifty guys who saw me."

They stared at one another for a moment.

"Why do you want to know where I was?"

"Because I've got a falcon missing."

"What? You mean the thing finally took off on you? Serves you right, you ask me."

"No kidding. That kind of attitude is what worries me."

"What happened?"

"The bird flew over a ridge about a quarter mile away from me and I heard a shot. I was tracking him but I lost the signal."

"And you're saying you think I had something to do with it."

"The thought has certainly crossed my mind."

"I'm not that stupid, Toronto. I know the federal regs."

"I'm sure you do." Toronto chuckled. "Just like you know the federal regs about pot growing."

Wylie held up his hands. "Listen, man. I don't want any hassles. You and I don't see eye to eye about a bunch of stuff. But I didn't mess with your bird. And I wouldn't, you dig? Like I said, I was working here all day. You can go ask anyone."

"Trust me. We will."

"You want anything else from me? Cause I need to get back to work here . . ."

"No," Toronto said. "That's all for now."

Wylie nodded and turned to go.

I began walking out with Toronto and Nicole.

"Hold on a sec," Wylie said behind us.

We turned back to him.

"I don't know why I'm doing this, Toronto, but now let me ask you something."

"What's that?" Toronto eyed him with suspicion.

"Where exactly did you say you heard this shot?"

Toronto described the location in detail. When he finished Wylie stood for a moment scratching his beard.

"You have something else you want to tell us?" Toronto asked.

"Yeah. Maybe." The young man glanced around. "Not here."

Toronto looked at him. "Okay. When and where?"

7

"What did you think?" Toronto asked me as the three of us drove away from the site.

"I think he was telling the truth."

"Me, too."

"He was acting a little squirrelly though at the end. Be interesting to see what else he has to say."

"Very interesting," Toronto said. We had made arrangements to meet Wylie over his lunch hour at a deli in town. It used to be a fancier restaurant and was the kind of place that served fresh sandwiches and had deep booths where you could sit and have a private conversation.

"Wylie was your prime suspect?" Nicole asked.

"Yeah."

"But you said you had more than one."

"Right. Next, we're going to talk to my former client."

"You mean the one who owns the land where Jazzy was shot?"

"Right."

"You think he could be our shooter?"

"Unlikely. But one of his ex-employees is a good bet. Dr. Clayton hired me to get rid of the joker about three months ago."

Toronto's former client, Dr. Ricardo Clayton was a former practicing physician, famous for his appearances and infomercials on TV about self-healing and nutrition. His books and DVDs had sold in the gazillions and he even had his own cable network, where he headlined the marquee show with his stunning wife, filling the rest of the programming with infomercials for vitamins, herbals, and other healthcare products. His net worth must have easily been in the hundreds of millions. I'd heard Clayton had moved to the region a couple years before.

"What did this employee do that made the doctor hire you to get rid of him?"

"Not he, she. The woman worked for him as a chef. Hot tempered, and not too bad to look at either. She was really upset with Clayton over some things he'd done to her, and Clayton was afraid she might try to poison his food or something."

"That hot-tempered, huh?"

"She could be."

"Why didn't Clayton just fire her then?"

"It's complicated. To tell you the truth, I think he was afraid of her."

"So he hired you to take the heat."

"My specialty."

We rode on in silence for a minute or two. Then Nicole said, "This what you do now, Jake, strong-arm people for a living?"

I felt her eyes on both of us. "Once in a blue moon," Toronto said. "If the price is right. Pays the bills."

"Doesn't exactly fit, you know, the back-to nature image."

"Uh-huh."

We were winding down a grade above a fast-flowing stream. The sky was bluer today, with cotton-ball clouds, and the air was less humid. The reprieve was only temporary, however. The weather people had predicted a typical summer afternoon buildup of heat with a chance of thunderstorms. A great day to be anywhere but here. Like at the beach.

We steered into another curve.

"So what are we hoping to learn from Dr. Clayton, then?" I asked.

"The chef didn't exactly leave me a forwarding address. I'll bet Clayton's sent her severance."

"When was she fired?"

"Two, maybe three months ago."

"She would have to be pretty peeved to take out your bird after all that time."

"Unless she's been planning it for a while . . . never should've let Jazzy get so far away from me, not this time of year anyway when we're not even hunting. We were only doing some lure training. Never thought he'd rake out on me like that."

"At least you had the transmitter on him. Otherwise, you might never have found him."

"Yeah," Nicole said. "But if Jake's right, the telemetry could have been what the shooter used to zero in on him too."

We all thought about that for a moment.

"Jesting hidden behind gravity," I said.

"Huh?" Jake said.

"Nothing. Something I read once . . . Guy was talking about irony."

"Whatever you say." He took the next right. We followed a long fence line until we came to a dead end, and then turned right again.

"This isn't the main entrance, is it?"

"No," he said. "That's about a half mile farther up the highway. But this is where we go in. Don't worry. The security people all know me."

We drove through a grove of birches, one or two of which sported closed circuit TV cameras. Around a curve we came to a guardhouse made of concrete and fieldstone beside an imposing wrought iron gate flanked by stone columns. We pulled up to the gate and Toronto rolled down his window. A man dressed in black wearing a headset came out. His face bore a wary look.

That changed when he saw it was Toronto. "Oh, it's you, Mr. T."

"Hey, Mike. Dr. Clayton home this morning?" "

"Sure is. He and the Missus went out riding earlier, but they never go for long. Ought to be back up to the house by now."

"You mind announcing us?"

"All right. Who're your friends?"

"Frank and Nicole Pavlicek. Private investigators from Charlottesville."

"You here on business, Mr. T?"

"Always." Toronto never fraternized with clients. It was a hard and fast rule with him.

The guard nodded, then wrote something on his clipboard before reaching down and turning a key in a console that caused the black metal gate to swing open. "Have a nice day," he said.

8

"Mr. T?" I gave Toronto a look.

He rolled his eyes and we drove on through the open gate, winding our way into dark forest again. The trees here were giant oak with the occasional bush and pachysandra as ground cover. I spotted a few more cameras discreetly tucked into the foliage.

"The main house is straight ahead," Toronto said. "We'll be coming into the employee parking lot behind the kitchen. The stables are around the other side of the main house. So are the tennis court, swimming pool, and sauna... You'll get to see the helipad though."

"No self-respecting country manor should be without one," I said.

We broke over a rise and the house appeared. It was stunning. Made of fieldstone like the guardhouse, with a slate roof and shutters painted a dark green. A stone terrace ran the length of the back of the structure, looking out on a lawn and a pond with a fountain.

A short man clad in tall boots approached as we pulled into the lot. His skin was tan. Black hair was beginning to gray around his temples, but otherwise he looked the picture of health. His mouth curved into a smile. He also had a royal air about him, one that only celebrity could bestow. I recognized him immediately as Ricardo Clayton.

The three of us stepped out of the Jeep. Toronto and Clayton shook hands.

"Jake Toronto," Clayton smiled. "Come down from your lair to mingle with the commoners?"

"We all have to sometime, I guess," Toronto said.

"How true." He stepped back and clapped his hands as if delighted with his former employee, before regarding Nicole and me. "And who might your associates be? Private investigators, from what I understand."

"This is Frank Pavlicek from Charlottesville and his daughter Nicole. Nicole works with her Dad."

"Charming. A pleasure to meet both of you."

He shook hands with the two of us as well. His grip was firm and radiated confidence, a practiced grip. He clasped my arm lightly with his opposite hand the way a politician might. I would have told him I'd seen him on television or that I enjoyed his books, except it wasn't true. I'd never read any of the books and I wasn't about to gush over a TV idol.

"Frank used to be my partner when I was a cop," Toronto said.

"Ahhhh, I see . . . well what can I do for you people this fine day?"

"I came to ask you a favor."

"A favor? Of course."

A woman emerged from the back of the house. At first, she appeared much younger than Clayton, with unblemished skin and blond hair that swept down her back. As she came closer, small, telltale signs that the dermatologist's laser couldn't erase revealed she was probably closer to the doctor's age. But she, too, looked radiant in her health. No casting director could have picked a better couple to advertise their natural health empire.

"Mr. Pavlicek. Ms. Pavlicek," Dr. Clayton said. "I'd like you to meet Sylvia, my wife. Jake, I believe you two already know one another."

The woman came forward. Like her husband, she was clad in riding boots and skintight pants as well, except that they more favorably displayed her willowy figure. A green windbreaker with an orange and black patch on one sleeve was draped around her shoulders. She slipped to the doctor's side and he put his arm around her. Her eyes seemed to dissect me as I shook her hand.

"So you were saying about a favor?" Dr. Clayton looked at Toronto.

"Right. If you remember, I keep and raise falcons, birds of prey, and the like."

"Yes, of course. Beautiful creatures. I gave you permission to hunt on our land. How has it been flying them on our mountain?"

"Great, thank you. Until yesterday morning, that is. Someone shot my peregrine falcon."

"Someone shot your bird on our land?" The doctor let go of his wife and folded his arms.

"I'm afraid so."

"Oh, what a shame," Mrs. Clayton's hand covered her mouth for a moment in surprise. "I'm terribly sorry. It must be a real loss for you." Her accent was lightly British and her stare was fixed on Toronto.

"That's awful," Dr. Clayton said.

"At least I think he was shot. The worst part is, I couldn't find any trace of him. He flew off on me. I was tracking him but then I lost him. I thought I heard the sound of a round being fired."

Which wasn't entirely true, of course. I looked at Toronto. One of the oldest detective tricks in the book was giving potential suspects false information, something they would have to act on in some way. Was Clayton a suspect? Did Toronto think he was still in contact with his former employee? Nicole and I made eye contact, but we remained stone-faced.

"No sign of the culprit either, then, I suppose," the doctor said.

"Nothing. But I heard the shot just before I lost the telemetry signal. The three of us will be heading back up to the area first thing tomorrow morning. If we can find the dead bird, maybe we can come up with some evidence that will point us to the shooter."

"Is there anything we can do to help?" Dr. Clayton asked. The physician seemed sincere. In spite of his money and celebrity and all, I already sort of liked the man. I supposed the millions who bought his books and watched him on TV liked him for the same reason: we all bought image. I wasn't sure what Jake was up to yet, but I would find out soon enough.

"Your old chef, Maria Andros," Toronto said. He had told me about her earlier. "She hasn't come around here again, has she?"

"No. You don't mean . . . you don't think Maria was involved in this, do you?"

"I don't know. But I'm not exactly at the top of her dance card, if you know what I mean," Toronto said.

"I know, but—"

"Have you been sending her any severance?"

"Of course, but that's just about come to an end."

"She's still in the area then?"

"As far as I know. She's moved, but not that far away. I think she works at the Homestead now."

"You have her new address?"

"I do. I have it in my files in the study. Would you like me to get it for you?"

"That would be great, if you don't mind."

"Of course. It'll only be a minute," he said. "Sylvia, maybe you could see if these gentlemen would like something to drink?"

"That's okay, Doc," Jake said. "We're fine."

"All right then." He disappeared into the house.

The mistress of the manor regarded us with calm eyes. "I feel terrible about your bird," she said. "I can't imagine why Maria would ever do such a thing."

"I hope she didn't," Jake said. "But she was pretty angry with me when she left your employ."

"Yes," Mrs. Clayton said. "But not that angry." She and Jake looked at one another for a few moments.

I shoved my hands in my pockets and leaned on the truck. "Did you know Maria Andros well, Mrs. Clayton?" I asked.

She tore her gaze from Toronto. "Maria? Oh, not that well. She only worked here for a few months."

"How did you happen to hire her?"

"Ricardo sees to all the employees. I believe she was referred by an agency."

"I understand she's quite an attractive young woman."

"Well, I . . . I suppose she is. That is if you–"

Sylvia Clayton stopped speaking and turned to look as her husband reappeared through the back door and strode toward us on the pavement. If she knew about the affair between her husband and Maria Andros, she wasn't making it obvious. She seemed even more upset about what had happened to Jazzman than we did.

Dr. Clayton handed Toronto a business card with the information written on the back. "You know, Jake," he said, "it occurs to me that if Ms. Andros was involved in any of this, she might be a threat to me or my family again. Do you think we need to reactivate our arrangement?"

"Not yet, sir," Toronto said. "Why don't you let us talk with her first?"

The doc seemed to think it over for a moment. "All right," he said. "You've still got my cell phone number?"

Jake assured him that he did.

We said our good-byes all around and climbed back into the Jeep. The doctor slipped his arm around his wife again. They waved as they watched us drive away.

9

I waited until we had cleared the guardhouse before speaking. "So what are we doing? Playing Agatha Christie here?"

Toronto smiled. "You might say that."

"I didn't come all the way over here to waste my time."

"You're right. No reason to be jerking your chain."

"Why are you feeding a setup to Clayton and his wife, too. You think one of them wasted your bird?"

"Not exactly." He lifted a hand off the wheel for a moment and scratched the back of his neck.

"Then what gives?"

He shifted in the seat. "You remember I told you this Maria had gotten into some difficulty with the Doctor and the Missus?"

"Right."

"Well, the specific difficulty had a lot more to do with the Doc than with his wife."

"Okay."

"He and the chef were having a fling."

So much for TV image. But certainly not a shock. I hadn't laid eyes yet on Maria Andros, but Sylvia Clayton, though beautiful, looked like she would give any man a run for his money.

"So why'd the doctor hire you then?" I asked.

"Because he wanted to break off the affair and the chef didn't."

"So he brings you in to find a reason to fire the chef."

"Uh-huh . . . Plus maybe give the young lady a reason to forget about him."

I looked across the seat at him. "What? Part of your job was to seduce her as well?"

He said nothing, drumming his fingers on the steering wheel.

"But I thought you said this Maria character hated you."

He shrugged. "Love. Hate. Two sides of the same coin."

Nicole sat up a little higher in her seat. "You slept with this woman, Jake?"

Toronto nodded.

"So you used her."

"If you want to call it that. Look, I was hired to convince her to leave her employer peacefully. It was a job."

"Some job," she said.

"Why didn't you tell us about this sooner?" I asked.

"I'm sorry, Frank. I should apologize to both of you. But I've developed a sudden case of doubt regarding Dr. Celebrity and I wanted to see what you thought without prejudice."

"What I think is the guy could charm tax money out of a libertarian . . . what I think is that he and his wife seem to be carrying on something of a show, and it makes me wonder what might be going on beneath the surface."

He nodded. We were both silent for a minute. He had the air conditioning on and the windows rolled up, so looking out from our shade on the bright Virginia landscape was almost like staring into one of those glassed-in exhibits at the zoo.

"Now that you've broken this chef's heart," Nicole said, "you think Clayton may have had second thoughts and gone back to whipping up some gourmet with her again?"

"Exactly what I've been thinking."

"The doctor likes the danger."

"Probably."

"And you're afraid he might tip off his on-again lover if we tell him what we've already found."

Toronto nodded. "That's pretty much the story."

"Guess there's only one way to find out," Nicole said. "Go see the girl."

10

Finding Maria Andros took us on a rolling thirty-minute drive along the Jackson River into Bath County and the village of Hot Springs. Hot Springs is a resort town tucked into the mountains, famous for its mineral baths, around which stands the Homestead Resort, a brick and glass cathedral to fine old Virginia living built around the turn of the century. There is a majestic ballroom and private bowling lanes for guests, a golf course and riding stables, and, in the winter, an outdoor ice skating rink and ski slope. There is even a falconry barn, where, for a fee, a licensed falconer will take guests on educational "hawk walks." Toronto and I have known the man who runs the operation for years.

Down the road from the resort we found the chef's address, a tidy frame house with flower boxes in the windows on the edge of the town near the stables. A blue Honda Accord was parked in the driveway. We stepped across the porch and rang the bell.

After maybe thirty seconds the door opened and there stood a striking young woman with short, dark hair. Her lips were full and glossy, her skin almost brown. Her violet eye shadow matched a sleeveless shell over cutoff shorts that made the most of her long legs.

"I don't want to see you," she said to Toronto.

"This is important," he said. "I wouldn't bother you otherwise."

She glared at him then scrutinized the three of us for a few moments, finally stepping aside to let us in.

"Who are these people?" she asked, gesturing toward Nicole and me.

"This is Frank Pavlicek and his daughter Nicole. They're private investigators. Old friends of mine."

"Old friends and real private eyes, huh? Perfect." She rolled her eyes. "You never cease to amaze me, Jake. What, did you folks come to try to Gestapo me out of my new job too?"

"Not at all," I said. "Mind if we sit down?"

"Why not?" She gestured toward a small living room. I took a rocking chair in the corner. Toronto sat on the large overstuffed sofa across from her. She crossed her legs; her toes were painted several different colors. "Forgive me for not offering high tea."

"I expect you get enough of that on the job," Nicole said.

Andros said nothing.

"You have a beautiful place here."

"I like it," the woman said.

"We'd like to ask you a few questions, if that's okay." Nicole was using her best sisterly voice. Not a put-on. It was genuine. We'd all agreed ahead of time that she should be the one to take the lead in talking to Andros.

"Go right ahead," Andros said. She kept glancing over at Toronto. "I'm listening."

"Did you know that Jake keeps falcons?"

"What? Those birds he hunts with? Sure, I know about them."

"Where were you yesterday morning about nine o'clock?"

"Yesterday? Here, asleep in bed. I worked late the night before."

"Were you alone?"

She peeked at Toronto again, then turned and stared at us, expressionless. "Yes, I was alone."

"I lost Jazzy," Toronto said. "Think someone may have taken him or even shot him."

Andros' eyes grew wide. She glanced out the window for a second.

"Do you know anything about it?" Nicole asked.

"Who, me?" The young woman laughed. "You're kidding, right?"

"You have to admit you were pretty upset with me last time I saw you," Toronto said. His monotone reminded me of how he used to question suspects in the Bronx. Had he felt something for this woman? It was impossible to tell.

She folded her arms. "Not enough to kill your stupid bird."

"We didn't say he was dead, Maria," Toronto said

"What?"

"I just said I thought someone shot Jazzy, but I didn't say he was dead. Can't find any trace of him, in fact."

"Well, I . . . Hey listen, I'm not into any of your dumb games."

"The Pavliceks and I will be going over that mountain again with a fine toothed comb at first light tomorrow," Jake said. "Sooner or later, we'll find Jazzy. Or what's left of him. We're not perfect, but we don't miss much. You'd be amazed what kind of evidence shooters leave behind."

Andros crossed her arms. "Go ahead. Knock yourselves out . . . Doesn't have anything to do with me."

"What about Dr. Clayton?" Nicole asked.

Her eyes grew a little narrower. "What about him?"

"Jake was flying Jazzy on his land when it happened. We went by to visit him earlier, which is how we found out where you were."

"So."

"Have you talked to the doctor lately?"

"No."

"Really?" Toronto, said. "You sure you and he aren't dancing a tango again?"

Andros spat out a grunt. "You've got some brass, Jake. After what you did . . ." She paused. She seemed about to cry and turned her head away for a moment to compose herself. "Why should I tell you anything about my life?"

Toronto looked embarrassed. When she turned back to us, her eyes brimmed with tears. They were beautiful eyes. There was no getting around that.

"You wouldn't object to being fingerprinted though, would you, if the sheriff up in Leonardston asked?" Nicole said.

"Why should I? Look, Jake, I didn't do anything to your friggin' bird, okay?"

Toronto rubbed his hands together. "Okay."

Andros stood, signaling an end to our interview. "Look. I've answered your questions. I'd like you all to please leave now."

"All right," Nicole said.

We all stood and moved toward the door. Andros followed. We were almost through it when she said, "Jake?"

He turned. "Yeah?"

"I hate what you did to me. In my book it makes you lower than low."

Toronto stood on the threshold of the apartment. He took in a deep a breath and let it out. "You're right," he said. "It wasn't the way I should have handled the situation. I was trying to do a job, but that's no excuse. I apologize. I used you and I was wrong."

Her demeanor shifted. "Like I said, I had nothing to do with it, but I'm sorry about what happened to your falcon."

Toronto nodded. "Me, too."

As we turned to leave I noticed a coat rack and a caddie for shoes beside the door.

No falcon feathers. No Frye boots. No smoking guns.

11

Gabriel Wylie came strolling in though the front door of Lord Alfred's Smokehouse and Deli in Leonardston a little after noon. The place was exactly the kind of hangout Toronto had described to us on the way over–retro seventies/eighties kitsch complete with a PacMan video game. The lunch counter was busy enough, with about a half dozen customers in the process of ordering or consuming already purchased sandwiches and drinks, but we weren't there for lunch. Wylie caught Toronto's eye and made a beeline for our booth.

"Thanks for coming," he said as he slid into a chair next to Toronto across the table from Nicole and me.

"You come here often, do you?" I asked, looking around some more. I was concerned about eavesdropping. This being a small town, someone might recognize Wylie and wonder what he was doing meeting with Toronto and a pair of investigators.

"Never," Wylie said. "It's why I picked here."

"Smart. What else do you have to tell us?" Toronto was in no mood for chit-chat.

Wylie glanced around the deli as if he wanted to make sure no one else was listening to him. "If I tell you guys something, you have to promise me you'll keep my name out of it."

"Done," I said. If we were talking about criminal activity, Wylie might be compelled to testify, but no need to burden him with that just yet, or slow him down when he seemed ready to talk.

He hesitated before lowering his voice. "What do you people know about illegal dumping?"

I looked him over. He was still in his work clothes but had cleaned himself up a little bit and combed his hair. I suspected the improved grooming had something to do with Nicole being there. Then again, his appearance upgrade might have had something to do with a genuine desire for doing good. "What kind of illegal dumping?" I asked.

He lowered his voice even further. "Wastewater."

"Water?"

"Yeah. When they drill in some of the mines a few miles from here, there's lots of wastewater produced, and they can't just dump it anywhere legally because it seeps into the groundwater and the watershed."

"So what does any of that have to do with my falcon?" Toronto asked.

"One of the guys I work with at the construction site drives a tanker truck part time for one of the big haulers around here. Normally, he dumps his wastewater loads at the treatment plant, but he told me a couple of weeks ago they sent him somewhere else to dump his load when the line got too long at the plant. Guess where?"

"Up where Jake lost his bird," Nicole said.

"Exactly."

"Are you saying he just dumped his wastewater load on the ground?"

"No, no. He said there was a pipe and a place to dump, except he wasn't sure what it was all about. He just thought it seemed a little fishy, that's all."

"So why'd he tell you?"

"Because he knows I care about stuff like that. I've been meaning to look into it some more, but I've been so busy lately on the job, I haven't had time."

"And this was still on Dr. Clayton's land?" I asked.

"Yeah. I'm pretty sure the doctor owns all of the land up that way. That's what all the signs up there say anyway–Clayton Farms."

"I still don't see the link to Jake's falcon," I said.

Wylie brushed a strand of hair back from his forehead. "Don't you get it? Maybe Toronto here was getting a little too close to somebody's illegal operation. Maybe the bird landed on their dumping station or something and they freaked when they saw that stuff you put on its legs."

"You mean the leather jesses and tail transmitter."

"Yeah, whatever."

Toronto leaned forward in his chair. "Okay. We'll look into it," he said. "Do you think we could get this guy to give us directions to where he dumped his load?"

"I've done you better than that." Wylie fished into the front pocket of his blue jeans. "Before I came over here just now, I got him to draw this out for me." He pulled out a crumpled packing list for construction supplies and spread it on the table. A crude map was drawn in blue ink on the back.

"You know if we find anything, your friend may have to talk to the state or federal authorities," Nicole said.

"Yeah, well, when you guys showed up this morning, I got to thinking about that. If there really is anything bad going on here, I figured maybe you folks were better able to look into this kind of stuff than me."

"And take whatever heat comes down," she said, staring at him.

Wylie looked back at her for a moment. I wondered if he got the fact that in Nicole's estimation he'd just dropped a peg or two. If he did, he wasn't about to show it. "Pretty much," he said. "I don't want this guy to lose his job over giving me this information . . . me neither." He turned and looked at Toronto and me.

"If what you're saying is true, Mr. Wylie," I said. "Losing your job may turn out to be the least of your worries."

"What do you mean?"

"Dr Clayton seems like a civilized guy. But illegal haulers generally don't look too kindly on whistle-blowers."

"Hey. That's why I came to you people. This is the kind of thing you do for a living, isn't it?"

Toronto, Nicole, and I all exchanged glances around the table.

"It is indeed," Toronto said.

12

A small sign marked the turnoff from the main highway onto the dirt road shown on the truck driver's crudely-drawn map. Posted signs hung at intervals along a wire fence told us we were still on Clayton Farms land. The early afternoon sun baked the earth like a brick oven. Nothing moved in the woods but insects.

The road ended at a small storage building beside which stood the capped drainpipe the truck driver must have been talking about. No one was dumping water now. The place looked deserted. It didn't exactly look like the type of enterprise someone would shoot a bird over, no matter how motivated they might have been to prevent discovery.

The three of us climbed out of Toronto's Jeep as we pulled up next to the building.

"Not much here," Toronto said.

I watched as he examined the door to the building. "I've always admired your facility for understatement."

He continued looking over the door. "It's locked and it's alarmed."

Nicole stepped up beside me. "Any way to disarm it?"

Toronto frowned. "Not easily."

They started talking about circuit boards and digital mumbo-jumbo.

I stepped back and took a look around. Was a dead bird, the sketchy testimony of an unseen truck driver, and a lock and alarm in the middle of the woods probable cause enough to call for help? Not really.

"Hey guys. How about this for an idea?"

Toronto and Nicole turned to look at me.

"Let's just break-in and trip the alarm," I said.

"What?" Nicole looked horrified. "You give us enough time, we can probably disarm this thing."

"'Probably' isn't good enough. I, for one, don't care to sit around here all day. And what's the worst that can happen? Jake here is on good terms with the owner and has permission to be on this land. We can always explain we were just following up on a lead over the bird shooting, and we're all armed in case something worse should happen."

Jake began to nod his head. "Makes good sense to me. I've got a sledgehammer and a couple of crowbars in the back of the Jeep."

"We'll have to pay for any damage to the door, of course, but maybe the good doctor will show mercy on us."

Nicole continued to look at me like I had a screw loose. "Men," she said, rolling her eyes. "No use thinking through an elegant solution to a problem when you can just use brute force."

"Exactly." I smiled.

Toronto smiled back, and less than three minutes later we had the door open with a broken console hanging by a tangle of wires to one side with its panel blinking. Pulling the door back, we stepped inside.

"Well, that was pretty much a waste of good muscle," Toronto said.

The small structure was completely empty except for a clipboard hanging on the wall with a sign-in sheet and a list of drop-offs made by tank truck drivers. Affixed to a bulletin board beside the clipboard a large official-looking placard printed with both state and federal seals indicated we were standing in a one hundred percent government approved dumping station—most likely surplus storage for the waste processing plant down the road for use when the plant got too backed up. In addition to breaking and entering, we'd probably just broken at least a half dozen federal laws.

"Great," Nicole said.

"Ouch," I said.

"So much for Gabriel Wylie's dumping conspiracy theory."

"Looks that way," Toronto said. "But it was worth checking out."

"You think Wylie set us up?" I asked.

"Would make things interesting, wouldn't it? Except I don't think he's that smart."

13

Two Clayton Farms security men showed up in a Range Rover as we were trying to put the shed door back together. They weren't exactly amused. Nor were they sympathetic with our cause, until we offered to follow them back to the house to talk to Dr. Clayton. Toronto's presence also seemed to pacify them. Apparently, like the guard at the gate, they'd had enough dealings with him in the past to rest assured that we weren't up to no good.

This time, we were ushered through a side door into the great house itself. Mrs. Clayton must have been out because I overheard one of the security types talking about her being in town for the afternoon. Dr. Clayton was at work in his study, seated at his desk staring at a pair of oversized computer screens, a black windbreaker draped over the top of the tall seatback behind him. The office also featured a theater size movie and video conferencing screen as well as a wall full of smaller video screens. Not to mention a small television studio with Clayton's impressive library serving as backdrop. There was a mobile television camera, overhead boom mike, and equipment for satellite uplink. Clearly, we had stumbled into the never center of the Clayton empire.

Our escorts made themselves scarce as soon as we were ushered into the room, closing the office doors behind.

"Jake, I understand there's been some kind of problem up at our dump site." Clayton barely looked up from his work.

"That's right, Doc. And I'm sorry to have to tell you we're the problem."

"Oh?" Now Toronto had the man's attention. He looked over top of his reading glasses before squinting back at the screens and clicking something with his mouse. Then he pushed his chair away from the desk and stood up. "How is it you're the problem?"

"We broke into the shed."

"You broke into my shed?"

I stepped forward. "We did and we're sorry. It was my idea. We'll pay, of course, for any damage to the property."

Clayton focused on Toronto. "Is this still about your missing bird?"

"That's right," Toronto said.

"I know your falcons are quite capable creatures. But I didn't think one was so skilled he could pick a lock and bypass a security system in order to hide out in a shed."

"You'd be surprised, sir." Toronto smiled, trying to lighten the moment, but Clayton wasn't buying.

"But you didn't find anything in the shed, did you?"

"Nope. Looks like whatever operation you've got going up there is on the up-and-up."

"Did you seriously think I would be involved in something that wasn't?"

Toronto shrugged. "There's always a first time. And I've been surprised before."

"I have an agreement with the state and federal authorities. You're welcome to take a look at all the paperwork if you'd like."

Toronto waved his hand. "Won't be necessary."

"Do you suspect me of doing something to harm your bird, Jake? Is that it?"

"Not exactly."

"What does that mean—'not exactly'?"

"It means everybody's a potential suspect until I find out who did it." Toronto wasn't backing down.

"What about my security guards? It could have just as easily been one of them."

"I suppose so."

The doctor turned his attention on me. "Do you normally break into buildings in the course of your investigations, Mr. Pavlicek?" he asked.

"No," I said. "We usually call in our SWAT team for that."

"Your what?"

"I'm kidding. Look, we care about what happens to our birds. They fly for us and bond to us. We owe it to Jazzy to find out what happened to him. That's why Jake's going so overboard on this."

Clayton looked back at Toronto. "But you can always get another falcon. It's just a bird, isn't it?"

"Not to me," Toronto said. They stared at one another for a moment.

Clayton finally nodded. "All right. I'm going to let this pass. I didn't shoot your bird, Jake. I can assure you of that. I enjoy a good hunt now and then, just like you people do, but shooting anything illegally is wrong, and it's not something I'd ever engage in."

It was my turn to nod. I wasn't sure I totally bought his story, but he garnered a lot of points by not calling the law on us.

He looked over the three of us. "Sylvia and I have built a pretty good life here," he said. "Things are going very well with our various businesses and television network. We love the countryside. Most days, it makes me happy to just get up in the morning. There are times I even feel like one of your birds must feel, like I'm flying."

He was laying it on pretty thick. I couldn't help but wonder why.

"But you've had some issues with Mrs. Clayton, haven't you?" I asked. I wanted him to know I was fully aware of the circumstances surrounding the situation with Maria Andros.

Clayton hunched forward in his chair. "Sylvia and I have had our differences from time to time, that's true." He folded his hands across the blotter on top of his desk. "But what couple hasn't?"

It was hard to argue with his line of logic.

"How long have you been married?" Nicole asked. I noticed she'd pulled her smartphone from her pocket and was holding it loosely at her side.

"Five years. My first marriage ended in divorce."

Toronto stepped forward "I'm very sorry we broke into your shed, Dr. Clayton. I respect your property. We won't make that kind of mistake again."

Clayton leaned back in his chair. "It's all right. No real harm done. Like I said earlier, I hope you find your falcon or whoever took him."

We exited the mansion no worse for the wear.

Outside, on the bluestone patio that ran the full length of the house, Sylvia Clayton lay on a chaise in the sun. She was an attractive woman. Her leopard skin bikini left little to the imagination, and I was having visions of Marcia at the beach again.

"I see you're back to harass us, Jake Toronto." Mrs. Clayton smiled from behind her oversized sunglasses as she rolled to her side and propped on an elbow to take a look at us.

"Yes, ma'am."

"Is this about that falcon of yours again?"

"I'm afraid so."

She shook her head and made a face in disgust. "I hope when you catch whoever did it you give them what's coming to them."

"That's our plan."

"Mrs. Clayton?" Nicole stepped forward. "Do you mind if I ask you a question?"

"No, dear. Of course not."

"Were you here the other day? . . . I mean, the afternoon Jake lost his bird?"

"Yes, I was. I was in the house most of the day. Then I spent some time picking blackberries. We have a fair number of bushes along the edges of the fields and our new chef makes these incredible blackberry pies."

"Did you hear anything that sounded like a shot being fired?"

"That afternoon?"

"Yes."

Mrs. Clayton shook her head. "I'm sorry. I'm afraid I didn't hear anything of the sort."

Nicole let out a sigh and nodded.

"Was my husband able to be of any more help?"

"A little. He's been very generous and understanding."

"Well," Mrs. Clayton beamed again from behind her glasses. "That's just the type of person he is."

"It certainly seems that way."

The matron of the manor rolled onto her back again, her face reaching out for the sky. "Anyway, I hope you people get your man."

As we left in Toronto's Jeep, Nicole began punching buttons on her smartphone.

"You got something?" I asked.

"Yes. Did you notice the jacket draped around the side of Dr. Clayton's chair in his office?"

"Sure. I noticed it."

"I snuck a picture of it with my phone." She pulled the photo up on her screen and showed it to Toronto and me, zooming in on the sleeve.

"How about that patch on the shoulder," Toronto said.

"I saw it," she said. "Didn't know what it was, though. Do either of you?"

I examined the patch in the photo more closely and nodded. "That windbreaker belongs to a competitive marksman," I said.

14

The Affalachia Rod and Gun Club was a rustic affair, a post and beam main structure with a patchy shingled roof. The place looked quiet, almost deserted in the blazing heat of the day.

The proprietor's name was Simmons. We found him perched at a table inside the front door cleaning a shotgun, a large tumbler full of Johnny Walker resting close at hand. He looked to be in his mid to late fifties with a red face, a bulbous nose, and a shock of silver hair swept to one side. His world-weary eyes were frozen gray-blue.

"Mr. Simmons?" I asked.

The man looked up form his cleaning. "You got him."

"Wonder if we might ask you a few questions."

"Yeah? And who might you be?"

"My name's Frank Pavlicek. I'm a private investigator from Charlottesville, and this is my daughter and business partner Nicole."

"Private investigators, huh?" He took up his cleaning again, sliding a thin brush down the barrel. "Got some sort of ID?"

I took mine from my wallet and handed it over. Nicole gave him hers as well. Simmons made a show of examining them while he cleaned. He looked back and forth between the ID and Nicole a couple of times, almost as if he recognized her from when she was a teen in Leonardston years before.

"Y'all from Charlottesville, I see."

"That's right."

"What brings you way over here to our neck of the woods?"

I explained our situation in general terms and what had happened to Toronto's falcon.

"Toronto? Y'all are friends with Jake Toronto?"

"That's right."

"Well, why didn't you tell me that up front?" He put down his gun and shook our hands. "Any friend of Jake Toronto's is a friend of mine. You people go ahead and come on in the back."

A smile covered his grimace as he pulled himself from his chair and began to limp across the floor, leading us toward an open doorway that led to a much larger clubroom. He must have seen me staring at his gimpy knee.

"Got this in Desert Shield," he said. "Took shrapnel and a 7.62 mm round courtesy of Saddam's Republican Guard. Jake will tell you. Him and me go way back."

I nodded.

"So something happened to one of Jake's birds, huh? And I'm guessing since you're here you're thinking someone shot him."

"That's pretty much the situation. But this is not a slow bird. If he was in a stoop when they shot him, we're talking over two hundred miles per hour."

Simmons scratched his chin. "Be like shooting a missile diving straight down. Not many folks could make a shot like that."

"No, sir. And we couldn't help but notice when we were in Dr. Clayton's office out at his farm earlier this afternoon that he had a competitive marksman's patch on his windbreaker."

Simmons nodded. "Clayton's a marksman, no doubt about that. He and some of the people from his farm are out here a couple of times a month for practice. Sometimes he even brings his wife along. He likes shooting sporting clays, too, from what I hear."

"So you think he could've made such a shot?"

"Probably. But he's not the only one around here might've pulled it off. Hell's Bells, with the right rifle I could've maybe hit the thing myself."

"You have a lot of folks coming in here who could've made it?"

"Now, I didn't say that. You've got to be in top form to pull off something like that. What I hear, Clayton doesn't just shoot here. He's got his own private range over there on his farm, too. Guess he comes over this way because he likes the socializing and the variety. If he shoots over there, too, well, I'd say he's in pretty top form."

"So we should still consider him among our top suspects."

"Assuming your bird was shot, I'd say so."

15

The tractor-trailer tanker bore down on Nicole and me as we drove back to Toronto's. We were on the two-lane highway that curved around the mountain. I had the Ford at the speed limit, maybe even a couple miles per hour more, a reasonable speed. The big rig appeared in my rearview as if from nowhere. The cab was a Peterbuilt, but in the late afternoon glare from the sun, I couldn't make out much more in my mirror. Whoever was driving the rig must have really been pushing the edge on those curves.

"Dad," Nicole said, a note of concern but not panic in her voice, as she glanced in her side mirror.

"I see him." We'd hit an empty stretch of road still a couple of mile out of town. The roar of the tanker's powerful engine rumbled in on us like an approaching freight train.

I pressed down on the accelerator and watched the speedometer climb. The Ford jumped out ahead for a few moments.

But the tanker driver wasn't through. As we rounded a curve into a half-mile straightaway, the tanker came barreling on behind. Once he hit the straightaway, the driver must have shifted down a couple of gears. The tanker closed the distance between us. A small car approached in the opposite lane.

This was going to be close. The tanker must have been doing at least ninety as it grew larger and larger, filling my mirror, and the driver laid on his horn. A deafening wail. The small car was growing ever nearer. I could either speed up, trying to outrun the big rig, and take my chances of causing a wreck, or find a way out.

The shoulder looked wide enough. I waited until the last possible moment, angling my truck onto the shoulder out of the tanker's way as the tanker blew on past. The driver kept blowing his horn and the small car passed safely on the other side.

Braking to a stop in a cloud of dust left in the tanker's wake, I lifted my hands off the wheel. "That was interesting."

"That was not fun," Nicole said. We watched the big truck recede into the distance.

"The guy was nuts. You think he was running late for a delivery?"

"Oh, please." She rolled her eyes.

"You get a look at the driver?"

"Baseball cap, big sunglasses, and a beard. That's about all I could tell."

"You've just described over half of the truck drivers in Virginia."

"I know. I know."

"How about a plate number?"

"I made out a six and a two, but the rest of the numbers were covered in grease."

"He might get a citation for that, at least, if the Sheriff doesn't catch him for speeding."

"But that's not really the issue."

"No, it's not."

"You think it was some kind of message?"

"No doubt."

"But I thought you and Jake were cool with Dr. Clayton and his federal permit for dumping and all that."

"I thought so, too. But there must be more to it than meets the eye. Obviously, we were mistaken."

"We could've been killed, Dad."

"I don't think so. Not yet. If he'd really wanted to run us off the road, he could've done so easily enough around those curves. But someone is definitely trying to get our attention."

"You mean scare us off."

"That would be the idea."

Nicole took her sunglasses off and rubbed her eyes. One thing I knew: my daughter didn't scare easily. She wasn't about to back down now. "So what are we going to do?" she asked.

I sighed. "Check the load on our guns and make sure we're ready to go for whatever Jake has planned for tonight. If that guy Wylie wasn't barking up the wrong tree and Jake's peregrine getting shot is somehow mixed up in what just happened with that tanker, things ought to be coming together soon enough."

Nicole shook her head. "I think we may be missing something. Something to do with Maria Andros. She knew stuff she wasn't telling us."

"Andros and the Claytons, and even Wylie–I wouldn't be surprised if they all do."

16

The female goshawk was only a few months old, Toronto explained, and still in her immature plumage. I'd flown a couple of red-tailed hawks, had a short stint with a Kestrel, and currently flew a Harris Hawk, but I'd never handled a Gos before. Except for her coloring, she looked plenty mature to me. I could feel the power flow through her talons as she squeezed against my glove, her almost orange eyes fixed on mine. She had a rounded back and a bold white eyebrow, and was still mostly brown up top, although Toronto said this would eventually turn a bluish-gray. The grey ghost, as Goshawks were sometimes called. Toronto had named her Jersey.

Earlier, Toronto had taken Nicole and me through a little album of photos he'd taken of Jazzman too. In life his peregrine falcon had been magnificent: huge black eyes, steel-blue head, back, and wingtops, black and white stripes underneath. Peregrines were the fastest creature on earth, and in a vertical dive, called a stoop, could reach speeds well over two hundred miles per hour.

Nicole was still flying an RT, but she'd always longed to have a peregrine. "I can see why you'd be so upset," she said looking through the photos.

"Jazzy was a good one, no doubt about that." Toronto closed the book shut as we came to the end of the pictures. He rarely grew emotional, but the hitch in his voice betrayed his feelings over having lost something so precious, especially to someone taking it away violently, a rage tinged with deep sadness.

He slipped on his own glove, took Jersey from me, and carried her back to her perch inside her mews.

"What time we leaving for the mountain?" I asked.

"A little after eight. I want to be in position before dark."

"And Sheriff Daveys is coming, too?"

"That's what he told me."

"You really think someone will show?"

He shrugged. "That's what I'm betting. Except for what you told me about Simmons and the shooting club, no one besides the vet school people knows for sure Jazzy was shot and killed. We've dropped enough hints with all of our suspects to make them believe we'll be scouring the mountain tomorrow."

"Any hard evidence?"

"Not really. But what else do we have? Daveys said Clayton's prints from his business card didn't match the ones on the battery."

"That would've been too easy," Nicole said.

While Nicole and I were talking to Simmons at the shooting club, Toronto had hijacked the sheriff again for a few minutes outside his office and explained our plan. In a word, the sheriff thought we were all nuts. The fingerprint from the battery hadn't matched any in the FBI's criminal database up in Clarksburg. The only reason Daveys even entertained the idea of heading up a mountain in the dark with the three of us was his debt to Toronto. But Toronto said the Sheriff perked up a little during a follow up phone call after hearing what we'd told Toronto about our encounter with big Tanker truck. Apparently, Wylie wasn't the only one with suspicions about illegal dumping.

"You're sure the chef and the doc and his wife are the only ones who could've stolen your other tracker?" I asked.

"Absolutely," Toronto said. "Not too many people know enough about my business to have pulled off the theft. The Claytons do because we're neighbors and I've worked for them."

"But they had no motive to kill Jazzy unless there's something to this dumping thing. And even then, it's a pretty thin thread."

"Right."

"And Maria Andros knows you and has a motive, except–"

"Except, hotheaded as she is, she's no killer."

"You said it. I didn't."

"You think we're going in circles?" Toronto asked.

"I don't know. Nicky and I were talking about it earlier. There's something here we can't quite put our finger on, and that bothers me . . ."

Toronto turned to my daughter. "What do you think it is, Nicky?"

"I don't know either," she said. "I'm still suspicious of both Andros and the Claytons. You really think someone is going to show up on that mountain tonight?"

"We've dropped enough hints, planted enough seeds."

"Let's just hope one of them decides to sprout," I said.

"I think we'll see some action," Toronto said. "And even if we don't, what's the worst that can happen?"

"The worst that can happen is that some random, beer-soaked hunter from Minnesota or somewhere downed your poor falcon. While we're wasting our time, the guy could be across five state lines by now and probably hasn't given it a second thought since."

17

It was cooler later up on the ridge. The night closed in like a dark anger, the bloodthirsty mosquitoes in full temper.

"You folks have got to be certifiable," the sheriff said as he helped us take down the floodlight stanchions and clean up the remnants of Jake's crime-scene investigation. The man's face was still beet-red and coated with sweat from the climb.

None of us was expecting much, but we at least we were well armed–Jake, Nicole and I with our handguns, the sheriff with his own plus a pump action shotgun. We concealed ourselves and settled in to wait.

A quarter moon rose slowly above the mist and after a while stood high over the clearing. The wind stirred the branches of the trees. It was a beautiful night for doing anything but staking out a mountain.

By one a.m. I was almost ready to call it quits. The sheriff looked antsy, too–he'd already disappeared to relieve himself in the bushes more than once. Nicole remained stoic, but even she was growing tired, I could tell. Toronto, on the other hand, barely seemed effected. In fact, he barely moved and might've been asleep, except that his eyes were wide open and constantly scanning the dark.

I was just about to say something about leaving when a pair of headlights appeared down the mountain.

"Someone's on the fire road," Toronto said calmly.

"Well, I'll be . . . ," the sheriff said.

Another pair of lights became visible in the same spot, and then vanished.

"Whoever it is, they have company," I said.

We all dug in a little deeper and waited. The sheriff made a show of checking the load on his weapons.

Twenty minutes later, I spotted two flashlights making their way up the ridge below us. I pointed.

"I see them," Toronto whispered.

"Nobody comes up here in the dark like this unless they're up to no good. We'll wait until they reach the clearing, then take 'em into custody," the sheriff said.

"Don't you want to see what they're up to first?" I said under my breath.

He stared at me for a moment, and then nodded his okay. The sound of twigs snapping and boots pushing through leaves reached our ears. These people weren't worried about making a racket. A woman's laugh floated through the air, but it didn't sound genuine. Instead, it carried a hint of fear.

A few moments later the lights popped into view on the far side of the clearing. Two ghostly figures stepped into the pale moonlight. It was hard to tell for sure, at first. But then it became clear that one held a rifle to the back of the other.

"Now, darling," a woman's voice said, "we're going to take a good look around and find that dead falcon before that big Indian or his two private eye lackeys find it first. I only hope some bear hasn't made off with it. I know you'll cooperate, dearest. You've always been good before."

"I'm getting pretty sick of this crap, Sylvia." The new voice belonged to Maria Andros. "You said you had to meet me up here tonight. Just the two of us. What's with the gun?"

"It's just a little gun, pumpkin, just for safety," Mrs. Clayton said. "It's a fun game though, isn't it?"

"Not for me."

We still held the element of surprise. With my head and eyes I motioned to Toronto to move around to one side of the pair while Nicole went to the other. The sheriff and I would take the middle.

I crept around to position myself behind a pair of boulders. The two women were moving toward Toronto's position opposite me now, sweeping their lights back and forth.

"You're jealous of Jake, aren't you?" Maria said. "That's why you killed his bird."

"Me jealous of Jake Toronto? What for? He was just being paid to get rid of you for Ricardo. Ricardo was the one who was jealous of you and me, dear. You must know that's true."

We heard only the night sounds for several seconds.

Then: "I'm not sure I want to do this anymore, Sylvia . . ."

Sylvia Clayton moved closer to Maria Andros, angling the barrel of the rifle toward her head. "You're tired, darling. We'll talk this over." She began to stroke the younger woman's hair. "That falcon was such a beautiful wild thing, you know. Did I tell you it was spiraling upward when I finally found it? The wings weren't even moving. I think they ride the currents or something. It was really quite a shot."

So Jazzman hadn't been shot in a stooping dive after all. Now that we had the perpetrator right in front of us, it all made sense. Apparently, Dr. Clayton wasn't the only one practicing his shooting out at the range.

"Ringing up." Toronto's voice punched through the darkness like an invisible knife.

The two women spun in his direction.

"When they rise like that," he said, "they ring."

The beam of Sheriff Daveys's flashlight illuminated the couple. "Hold it right there, ladies. It's the sheriff."

As if he'd been their shadow, Toronto seemed to materialize next to Mrs. Clayton and took hold of her arm and the rifle. Maria tried to turn from the light, but ran straight into me. She scratched my face, tried to bite my shoulder, and kicked at my ankles.

"It's okay," I said, with Nicole's help holding her at arm's length. "It's okay now . . . It's over."

In a minute it was, with the sheriff reading the handcuffed Sylvia Clayton her rights while Maria Andros heaved sobs into Nicole's shoulder.

"This is absolutely ridiculous," Mrs. Clayton said. "I'll have all of your jobs for what you're doing here."

"All due respect, I don't think so, ma'am," the Sheriff said.

"Do you have any idea what my life has been like the past couple of years? All the money we've risked with the network. I told Ricardo we should have gotten a divorce long ago, but we've been trying to hang on until the show goes into syndication. The cable rights could be worth millions, or we could lose everything we've worked for. Don't you people understand?"

The Sheriff seemed unmoved as he turned with another set of handcuffs for Maria Andros. Apparently, he wasn't an investor.

"Don't you dare say a word, Maria," Mrs. Clayton tried to lunge at the younger woman, who seemed too traumatized to care. "And I'm not saying anything else either. I want to talk to my lawyer."

The Sheriff finished reading both of them their rights.

I made eye contact with Toronto, who was examining Sylvia's rifle. "Private eye lackeys, huh?"

He shook his head and smiled.

18

The next day Toronto, Nicole, and I buried Jazzman in the high clearing. It was a private ceremony, just the three of us beneath a pale blue sky.

A lot still needed sorting out after conversations at the jail the night before with Maria Andros and with Gabriel Wylie, who'd been rousted out of bed and brought in for questioning by one of the Sheriff's investigators. Turned out Sylvia liked to play both sides of the tracks. In addition to her erstwhile romantic advances toward Maria she had a boyfriend on the side who owned one of the local trucking companies. In an attempt to keep up her overly lavish lifestyle and fund the growth of her husband's TV ventures, they'd been double dumping waste water as Wylie had alleged, falsifying records. Whether Dr. Clayton knowingly participated in the scheme was unclear, but the Feds were being called in to help sort it all out.

I think Jazzman would have liked the spot Toronto picked out for his final resting place. A couple of yards from the edge of a cliff formed by a huge rock outcropping, where the sun slanted gold against the grass and the long view to the valley below would afford the falcon peace and security.

When finished, we descended to the fire road again. Toronto said he'd give Nicole a ride back to Charlottesville where he'd help her look in on our own birds and run a couple of other errands. A light breeze blew across the forest canopy as I pulled open the door to my pickup.

"Thanks for coming, Frank."

"At least we found out what happened."

"I blame myself."

"I know."

He and I shook hands and he gave me a bear hug. I hugged Nicole as well and waved as they saw me off.

Passing down the dirt road, I couldn't help but glance back up the mountain to the top of the cliff where we'd laid the peregrine to rest. I like to think that in some way, beyond our understanding, Jazzman still soars there on that precipice. Maybe the spirit that lived in him lives somewhere in us, too.

The road is long.

I would have five more hours of thinking to the beach.

END

Introducing
An Excerpt From

The Blue Hallelujah

by Andy Straka

*etective Jerry Strickland's wife Rebecca went
to prison after being convicted of killing one of
his suspects in a murder case. There she eventually
succumbed to cancer. Now, as the end of his own life
nears, it's time for the elderly Jerry to tell what really
happened with Rebecca and why. But when his eight-
year-old granddaughter Marnee goes missing the tale
takes a new turn. Jerry rushes to help in the search and
discovers that not only may Marnee be in peril, her
disappearance may point to a piece of Rebecca's story
that has been missing all along.*

Prologue

All afternoon the old man had been sweltering in the steamy woods, watching and waiting. All afternoon with a pit in his stomach, sweat dripping from his brow onto his dark clothing, flies and mosquitoes biting and swirling. He had lost track of how many times he'd raised the binoculars to his eyes, struggling to keep a focus on the girl.

Not much else was astir in the late afternoon heat.

Soon time would be running out. He glanced down at his watch. In a few minutes the camp would begin breaking up for the day and a line of parents in their cars would start forming along the entrance road. The girl, he knew from watching, could be a bit of a loner. Maybe he would be able to slip behind one of the restrooms and grab her without being noticed, but it would be a big risk.

He watched as the children were herded into loosely organized groups. Counselors only kept close track of the younger ones and near pandemonium ensued. Could he use the temporary confusion to his advantage?

He was just about to leave his hiding spot and move through the bushes down the slope when the unexpected happened. The girl broke off from her group and began moving in his direction alone.

He could scarcely believe what he was seeing. She was making it almost too simple for him.

A wave of paranoia roiled his stomach as he swept the lenses over the main building and the swarm of campers and counselors again to make sure no had seen the girl leave. He wondered if the police were filling the tree line opposite looking at him, but when he scanned the area with his field glasses he saw no sign of such a thing.

The old man fingered his satchel with the syringe and rope inside. His patience had finally been rewarded. Some things buried should stay buried. He zoomed in once more on the girl. She was nine years old, he knew, didn't seem to be in any hurry, pretty dark hair and skinny legs. Dipping in and out of his view, she began tossing stones as she went.

He reached down to pick up his bag. Just a few moments more and she would be close enough for him to make his move.

One

When you know you are dying, the world shifts into a pastel phase. All the tastes, sights, smells, and sounds of this life grow dull, washing like detritus onto some bone cold beach.

That's how I have always imagined it, at least.

Now that I am actually closing in on the end I realize I need a new set of suppositions.

Tears fill my eyes at the sight of a hummingbird outside. The toast and honey I washed down with my afternoon coffee never tasted so sweet. From somewhere down the block, I hear the music of a baby's cry, and even the roaring assault of my neighbor's leaf blower rings of an orderly and benevolent domesticity. Nothing bad should ever happen when you are feeling and–maybe for the first time–really seeing such things.

Lori sits with me in the waning heat of the day, her gaze straying out the bedroom window at the rose bushes her mother used to tend. The light plays tricks with her cheeks. Still pretty, but I can't help but notice the first signs of wrinkles around her eyes–shadows of things to come. The air smells of the lingering traces of Lori's unidentifiable perfume. Her chair creaks as she kicks off her shoes and stretches her feet, legs suspended in midair.

"What did you eat for lunch today, Dad?"

She must have a million better things to do than hang around here with her old man.

"I'm sorry, what did you say?"

"You heard me."

"Would you believe beet, string bean, and cauliflower soufflé?"

"Hardly."

I smile, focusing on the quilt that covers my legs, double wedding ring pattern, one of Rebecca's many family heirlooms. Perched on the edge of the dresser, my antiquated television plays something softly in the background. "Guess I'm not the only keen-eyed detective in the room."

"And getting more keen-eyed by the day. You've been eating more of that leftover pizza, haven't you?" Her gaze bores into mine.

"Pizza? What pizza?"

"Da-ad . . . You know there's way too much sodium in that crap."

"Sodium, schmodium." I used to be much better at playing this game when I was a cop.

"You've got to start keeping a closer eye on your food intake."

"You sound like some nutritional brochure."

"You know what I mean." Her voice grows quiet as she adjusts her skirt, picks up a paperback book from the bedside table.

She works at the public library now. Books have become her thing. She needs more time to get used to my unavoidable passing. To lose your last remaining parent is no easy thing.

"Whew." Lori begins to fan the side of her face with the book. "It's hot in here. How do you stand it?"

"I don't know." I shrug. "It's not so bad."

She must wonder if my brain is beginning to deteriorate too. A stubborn old farm boy who grew up minus the comfort of cool inside air, I've taken to turning off the house air-conditioning and throwing open the windows all day to better appreciate the distant hum of traffic that floats through my Richmond West End neighborhood. Lying in wait for the tail of the occasional breeze, the smell of newly mown lawns. Lori starts to snicker, but catches herself in mid-sentence as if she needs to stifle any hint of cynical inevitability, the divided coda at which we seem to have arrived in our relationship.

"You have another doctor's appointment the day after tomorrow, remember," she says.

"I know. You don't need to remind me." I glance over her shoulder at the fading display of get-well cards on my dresser. A gift from some of my criminal justice students at VCU, it looks like it's suffering from some kind of time warp.

Lori's gaze wanders toward the open window again.

"Something is bothering you," I say.

"What?"

"Something has you worried, I can tell."

"No, Dad, I–"

"C'mon. Spill it."

She manages a tired half-smile but says nothing.

"You and Alex have another blowup?"

Alex, the father of my two grandchildren, has a law degree from the University of Virginia and a lucrative practice defending well-to-do criminals to show for it. He and Lori have been married for nearly eighteen years but are "presently estranged", as the polite like to put it. A couple of months ago Alex moved by himself into a fancy new condo downtown.

I began my career years ago with a modicum of respect for criminal lawyers and all that they go through to earn their education, not to mention uphold their end of the legal justice system. But that opinion has eroded over time. Alex hasn't exactly been a boon for the lawyerly cause.

"No, Alex isn't the problem," Lori says. "Not right now at least." She hesitates, glances down at her hands. "I think I'm a failure as a mother."

"What? What would make you say that?"

She shakes her head again and pulls her hand away.

"You're not a failure," I tell her. "You're one of the best mothers I've ever known."

It's Lori who has cooked breakfast for her two kids every morning for the past seventeen years, Lori who packs the school lunches, writes out the cards and wraps the birthday presents, fills out the school forms, shows up at the games and recitals and PTA meetings. She may not be the most organized person in the world, but I've watched her for years, and I know about the compromises she's made. She has her mother's heart. She has her mother's eyes.

"Is Marnee okay?"

Barney Marnee, as her older brother Colin still likes to call her. Eight going on nine years old and not so little anymore. I still hang onto this image of Marnee when she was a toddler, jumping out of Alex and Lori's car after it has pulled into the driveway, skipping down my walkway breathless with excitement—and I, rock-bound by an inability to show emotion, not knowing which way to turn until Marnee rushes into my arms. Something catapults time in that moment, pushing it to a spectacular radiance, like dancing, or make-believe kisses on the moon.

"Marnee's fine," Lori says. "The problem is Colin."

"Oh . . ." I nod as if I really know anything anymore about teenagers. "Colin again."

Sad to say, but I've been expecting trouble with my grandson. Colin isn't a bad kid, compared with a lot I've seen. But unlike his sister, whose bond with her mother seems to be insulating her from the effects of the pending divorce, Colin has taken the parental breakup like a knife to the heart. He masks the pain the way any seventeen-year-old might, with an I don't care attitude and occasional up yours kind of comment that in my father's day would have earned him a back-of-the-hand clip across the mouth. To anyone really paying attention, the hurt leaks out of him like an oozing wound.

"You catch him smoking pot again?"

Lori shakes her head. An errant strand of hair drops over her forehead and she twirls it nervously, an ancient echo, I remember, from her own long-ago childhood.

"What then?"

"We got into an argument last night. Colin told me he wants to move in with his father."

"Oh, he did, huh?"

The news is hardly a surprise. Alex, for all his many failings, has at least made an attempt to keep up his relationship with his son.

"The kid's crafty, you've got to give him that," I say. "You keep close tabs on him, but he knows he can get away with a lot more at his father's. You think he blames you for the separation?"

"Could be." She stares aimlessly into the sheet that is pulled taut against the mattress.

"Maybe I should have a talk with him."

"I can't ask you to do that, Dad. I mean—"

"Why not? It's perfect, you ask me. Maybe he'll listen for a change."

She says nothing.

"Tell you what. You bring him by and the two of us will have a little chat, man to man."

"Thank you," she says. ". . . I don't know what else to do."

For a moment, I can't help but see her as an adolescent again herself, balanced on the precipice between innocence and worldliness, the heart-darkening knowledge that no one in this world can make everything right. I think again of her mother, wishing I could somehow reach back in time for some of Rebecca's wisdom.

Lori's wireless phone burbles from inside her suit coat. She reaches for it on reflex.

I've grown to despise the things. They intrude on life far too much for my liking. Lori stares at the display.

"It's Colin. He's supposed to be picking up Marnee at her day camp out in Chesterfield." Looking annoyed, she pushes a button and welds the device to her ear. "Colin? Where are you?" She listens for a second. "You were late again? I keep telling you how important it is to be there on—"

She listens some more.

"What?" Her voice grows louder, registering anger mixed with something else, maybe fear.

I feel the need to move. I'm no invalid. Not yet, at least. I sit up and swing my legs off the bed.

The conversation goes on:

"What are you talking about?" Lori asks. More listening. "I want to speak to the camp director. Put her on the phone."

Something must be wrong with Marnee. Maybe she's sick of something. From the look on Lori's face, it isn't good. Lori slips her feet back into her shoes and, fumbling for her keys in her pocket, stands from her chair. "This can't be happening . . . not now," she mumbles. She smooths the side of her suit jacket.

Memories stir in me, cases and concerns long past. When Lori gets the director on the line, she proceeds to interrogate the woman about Marnee. Listens again. "Do you even know what is happening with the children under your care?"

I can make out the director's garbled female voice speaking into Lori's ear, but little else.

"No. Listen, I want you to go find her right now. Do you understand? She must be someplace. I'm coming over there." She disconnects the phone.

"What's going on?"

"I don't know yet."

"What do you mean?"

"They can't find Marnee at her camp."

Two

Hidden beneath a false bottom in one of the dresser drawers across from my bed, lies a thick sheaf of papers I have shown to no one–curled pages torn from a legal pad filled with my handwriting and bound together with a rubber band. I've been wondering if I should just go ahead and destroy the manuscript. Glancing at the top of the dresser, my thoughts race back to it now:

The Blue Hallelujah
A Memoir
By Jerry Strickland

The investigation that sent my wife Rebecca to prison started with fish. A lone fisherman on the James, at any rate, who caught more than he bargained for among the Belle Isle rocks: the partially decomposed body of a semi-nude young woman draped around a submerged log in sight of the Robert E. Lee Memorial Bridge.

The year was nineteen eighty-six. In the annals of homicide enquiries, no doubt many victims have been discovered in more exotic and colorful poses than Jacqueline Ann "Jackie" Brentlou. But the

Brentlou girl was only thirteen. She was from a stable, middle-class family in Woodland Heights, the youngest of three children, and she had disappeared one beautiful spring day while walking home from school.

That made her killing far from typical of the murders my partner, Edgar Michael, and I were working in Richmond at the time. Our typical caseload consisted of gang and drug-related murders, drive-bys involving out-of-town players who plied the I-95 corridor from Miami to New York trafficking heroin or cocaine.

Officially, that didn't make the Brentlou case more of a priority than any other. Unofficially, everyone involved, from the scene techs to the office of the Chief Medical Examiner, wanted in the worst way to find whoever was responsible killing Jackie Brentlou.

And find the killer Edgar and I did, if only too late. His name was Jacob Gramm and he had raped and murdered before. Rebecca was never able to tell the whole truth about how or why she came to know about and kill Gramm. Had she done so, she might have avoided spending the last six years of her life at the Virginia Correctional Center for Women.

During his summation at Rebecca's trial, the Commonwealth's attorney chose to gloss over Gramm's guilt. Instead, he had a lot to say about vigilantism and Rebecca's state of mind. It's only fitting then that I rise here at the end of my days to set the record straight. If he knew what I knew, even that Commonwealth's attorney would have to agree. Few have ever stood as falsely accused as my Rebecca . . .

Introducing
An Excerpt From

The Night Falconer

by Andy Straka

1

The war between birds and cats began when Dr. Korva
Lonigan, a respected physician and animal rights activist,
discovered a feather from a great horned owl with what she took
to be the remains of her missing tabby Groucho along the curb
in front of her apartment building on Central Park West.

I'm not making this up.

I never expected to become involved in a war between
species. Or between their human campaign managers, at any
rate. I never expected to return to New York City either, except
as a tourist. And if I had known that steamy Virginia afternoon
about the depths of survival and the spun-off fragments of a real
war we would end up unearthing, I might never have answered

the cell phone I'd stupidly left tucked in my shorts pocket while balancing two pounds of fidgety Harris' hawk on the back of my left hand.

I fished out the offending instrument with my free, ungloved mitt. New York City area code on the display. Maybe it was Pale Male, the famous red-tailed hawk, calling to be rescued from his unwanted celebrity status in Central Park. No such luck.

"Guess who," a female voice said.

My brain shifted into high speed reverse, flashing back nearly a decade and a half to a New York courtroom and a dark blue transit cop's uniform. The composed, coffee colored face of a character witness standing in for Jake Toronto and me, her arms crossed as she stared down the plaintiff's attorney in the thousand dollar suit who had helped engineer the wrongful death lawsuit against us.

"Darla Barnes," I said.

"Very good, Franco. I see you haven't lost your edge."

"I also have caller ID."

"Strange world these days, isn't it?" she said. "No such thing as privacy anymore. Just bought a new cell phone. Gotta remember to get this number blocked."

Darla Barnes was the only person in the world who had ever and would ever call me Franco. She'd earned that right one misty spring night in the Bronx when I was a newly minted NYPD detective and she, a mere transit rookie, had been instrumental in preventing me from being put under the knife by an over-zealous group of bikers at a dumpy watering hole near Yankee Stadium. For reasons different than my own, she'd been working the PI beat almost as long I had.

"It's been a while," I said.

"Yes it has. How's that little girl of yours?"

"Not so little anymore. She graduated from college a couple of months ago and is in the process of making the biggest mistake of her life."

"What's that?"

"Working for her old man."

Darla chuckled. "Pee-eyeing with you, you mean."

"You got it. How's your family doing?"

"Not as aged as yours of course, on account of my youthful grace and vigor. But my youngest, Sweetness, is the cutest little thing you could imagine and my ten year old, Marcos, is at the top his class in school."

"Great to hear it."

"Am I catching you at a bad time? You busy?"

"Not really. Nicky's got some programmer running a security audit on our network, so we're out of business for the afternoon. I'm just out here messing around with one of my birds."

It was late on a Friday, Fourth of July weekend. For the third day in a row, the mercury in Charlottesville had topped ninety-five degrees. We already seemed to be stuck in that interminable summer pattern of heat building through the day, followed by the break, somewhere in the afternoon, of a thunder-clapping downpour. Today's edition of cloudburst was running a little on the late side, however. The sun still did its thing. Inside my hawk's enclosure the air was as thick as oatmeal. My T-shirt felt like it had been super-glued to my back. Bits of fluffy down, cream and black, drifted through the chain link fence while Torch's talons danced nervously around my gloved fist.

"You mean to tell me you're flying one of your falcons right this second?"

"Not exactly. But I am holding onto a hawk in my other hand as we speak."

"Perfect."

"What do you mean?"

"You'll see . . . Got a job for you, Franco, if you're interested."

"Okay," I said.

In fact, it was very okay. Eagle Eye Investigations was sometimes flush with cash, sometimes not. Since our contract with a Northern Virginia security firm for post 9/11 background checks on federal hires had expired a couple of months before, 'not' was beginning to creep more into the equation.

"The client's name is Dr. Korva Lonigan. I'm calling you from her apartment in Manhattan."

"All right." The doctor was most likely having a problem with a piece of property or something she owned down here in central Virginia. Or maybe the issue involved a relative or an ex-husband, or an accident that had occurred in the area.

"I should warn you, though, Frank. This deal's probably a little different from the kind of work you're used to."

"How so?"

The last time I'd had work like that, six months before, I'd almost drowned at the bottom of a river while trying to figure out how to avoid getting blown to bits.

Darla was silent on the other end of the line for a moment. I adjusted my grip on the jesses and eyed Torch, who was now staring at me warily. Harris' hawks are native to the Southwest. Unlike me, my bird seemed to be doing just fine with the heat. He probably wouldn't even have minded had God decided to crank up the temperature another twenty degrees. There was no hunting for him this time of year, at least while he was in my care. He was too busy molting. All he basically had to do right now was sail around inside his enclosure to keep himself in some semblance of flying condition, eat, defecate, and make new feathers. Call it a wild hawk day spa. With the exception of deigning to interact with me for regular feeding and the occasional weigh-in, of course.

I decided I better tie him back on his ring leash. Torch squawked while I secured the line with a one hand knot and cast him off to fly up the wire onto his perch again.

"You still there, Frank?" Darla must have wondered if I was experiencing a medical emergency.

"Yeah, sorry, I'm listening." I backed away to lean against the fence, turning my head again into the phone.

"You want to know how this is different so let me ask you a question. Since you're so into birds and everything, people ever come to you with other animal issues?"

"I've dealt with a few animals who call themselves humans, if that's what you mean."

"I know that. But I'm talking about real live animals here. Criminal actions involving pets. Neglect, abuse, mutilation, killings—that sort of thing."

"Oh, no, can't say that I have. If I ever did, I'd refer it out to the SPCA, or if it were a wild animal, to Virginia DGIF or the feds at Fish and Wildlife."

"I see."

"Unless there was something more than just an animal problem going on of course."

"Of course."

"What, does this Dr. Lonigan have some kind of problem like that?"

"Possibly," she said. "Not exactly . . . ."

I waited, but she said nothing more, so I added: "A lot of times, you know, when you see animal abuse, it's just the tip of the iceberg. Intentionally inflicting harm on a domestic creature can be indicative of a whole host of issues."

"You mean like serial killers."

"That's one possibility."

"Okay, but look, hey, I don't think we're dealing with that kind of an issue here."

"Good. Because I'm out of the serial killer business."

She lowered her voice a little as if she were cupping her hand around the receiver. "This Dr. Lonigan comes from some very serious money. Prestigious job at Columbia. Hoity new place on Central Park West. You get the picture?"

"What kind of doctor is she?"

"Pediatric oncologist."

"Must not be easy work," I said.

"I'm sure it isn't."

"She married?"

"No."

"Children?"

"No."

"You said she's having some kind of problem with an animal though."

"Yeah. Hear me out, Franco. I don't want you to think I'm wasting your time here."

"It's all right," I said. "Spill it."

She breathed out a sigh, every bit as audible through our digital connection as if she'd been standing on the other side of the chain link across from me. "Dr. Lonigan wants . . . well. She wants me to hire you to help me find out what's happened to her missing cat."

Neither one of us spoke while I considered the possibility that a minor earthquake had just struck central Virginia, rendering some kind of momentary breach in the space-time continuum.

"I'm sorry," I said. "Did you say find her missing cat?"

"Yup."

"As in feline, alley cat, pet god or goddess?"

"You got it."

This was not exactly what I'd envisioned when Darla had mentioned a job. But presuming the missing kitty was still somewhere in New York State, at least I had an easy out.

Darla and I may both have been former NYPD and known New York, but in my case that had been so long ago Rudy Giuliani was still working as a U.S. Attorney. And as Darla must have very well known, I was only licensed to take on cases that initiated in the veritable Commonwealth of Virginia, or in neighboring states maintaining a reciprocal agreement with the Department of Criminal Justice Services in Richmond. New York was most definitely not on the list. Heck, for that matter, neither was Washington, D.C.

"Darla, you know I just can't¾"

"Hang on a minute. This is my case. You'll be working with me as a consultant."

I thought about that for a moment. Consultant did have a nice ring to it.

"And the client's authorized me to offer you double your usual rate, plus expenses," she said. "She's even got a vacant furnished apartment in her building for you to stay in and I can have a plane ticket waiting for at the airport first thing in the morning."

"What, no corporate jet?"

"Hey, I've seen people do a lot worse with their money, haven't you? And besides, there's a lot more to this than just a missing cat."

"Such as?"

"This woman is no flake. She thinks someone may have purposely killed her cat."

"Well, I'm . . . I'm sorry to hear that."

There is something particularly tragic about a dead domesticated animal. Death in the wild happens every second of every day—just look at my buddy Torch here, who knew without question what it was to have to kill in order to survive. But death actively brought inside the protective bubble of your home was another matter altogether. Still, I was having a hard time seeing myself as the next Ace Ventura.

Darla said nothing.

"I agree it's tragic, Darla. I just don't know if it's my kind of case."

"You said yourself if someone did this kind of thing to an animal it could be indicative of much bigger problems."

"Yes, I know, but—"

"It's the only pet the woman has ever owned."

"What kind of cat are we talking about?"

"Angora. Named Groucho."

Cute.

"But she's already hired you. Why does she need me?"

"Okay, here's what's been going on . . . At least two cats, one hamster, one guinea pig, and one puppy are now missing from her apartment building on Central Park West. The tenants have discovered what they think are fur remains for two of them, both of which were accompanied by the feathers."

"Feathers? What feathers?"

"Feathers from the tail of a great horned owl. Dr. Lonigan's had it verified by an ornithologist."

I was beginning to see where this was going. "Are you trying to tell me this group of people believes a wild great horned owl has somehow managed to take their pets from their building in the middle of New York City?"

"No, of course not. It's a newly renovated historic property, by the way. Grayland Tower. Did you see the pictures last month in the New York Times Magazine?"

"Sorry, no."

"Anyway, that's not the point. The issue here is the developer of the building. His name is Dominick Watisi."

"What about him?"

"Dr. Lonigan and some of the other apartment owners have been complaining for months about cost overruns with the construction and some other issues. Watisi refuses to even discuss the matter. The dispute escalated a few weeks ago when the tenants filed a lawsuit."

"Okay."

"Now it's made the tabloids, and Watisi isn't happy, you see? His company has another project on hold pending an upcoming bond referendum. There have been a couple of nasty public exchanges between Watisi and the tenants."

"You're saying Dr. Lonigan thinks this Watisi character had her Groucho whacked?"

"Looks that way. She's convinced he's hired a hit man who somehow got hold of an owl. They think this guy gets the pets out of the building, either at night or while people are away at work during the day, has the owl dismember them under the cover of darkness, and attempts to make the killings look like natural occurrences."

"Sounds pretty far-fetched if you ask me."

"C'mon, Frank. You've been around long enough to know that stranger things have happened."

"Maybe. But not very often. Big birds of prey have been known to kill cats once in a while. But it happens pretty rarely, and do you know how difficult it would be for even an experienced falconer, assuming he or she did have an owl, to purposely hunt with that bird in the middle of a city?"

"What about in Central Park in the middle of the night?"

"Anywhere, especially after dark. The whole thing sounds like the figment of someone's overworked imagination, if you ask me."

"Overworked or not, we're talking about burglary, murder, and cruelty to animals here."

"Does this Dr. Lonigan know I used to work in New York?"

"Yes, and she knows a little bit of your history."

"Then she must know some people up there may still think I'm damaged goods."

"She says she doesn't care about any of that."

"I assume someone's already tried contacting Humane Law Enforcement at the ASPCA?"

"Of course. They came out and investigated. Lonigan says they're concerned about the missing pets, naturally, but they refuse to take the idea about Watisi seriously. She even claims it wouldn't surprise her if Watisi's got some of the officials in his pocket."

"I doubt that. All these missing pets belong to people who are party to the lawsuit?"

"Almost. Four out of the five."

"Where did she come up with the falconry angle on the owl? I mean, besides there being the feathers and all."

"This is where it gets really interesting."

"I can hardly wait."

"They've had at least two confirmed sightings so far."

"Sightings?"

"One of the tenants in the building says he saw someone across the street in the park late at night from his balcony. Claims it looked like a small man swinging a rope over his head and a large shape swooping down at him from the shadows. Doesn't that sound like a falconer to you, Franco?"

"With a lure . . . maybe. Not exactly a prime witness though. In the dark, from that distance. He credible?"

"He swears that's what he saw . . . not only that, a security guard from the building now says she saw something too. She can't say whether it was a man or a woman, but the person was running away, wearing a long glove and carrying something big and gray and brown like an owl on it."

"Might just be some yahoo who happened to get hold of a bird."

"I need to let Dr. Lonigan know. Are you interested in consulting on this case, or not?"

"Maybe. Who'll be doing most of the legwork?"

"You, I'm afraid. It's still my case, but I've got a few other things on my plate at the moment."

"So you're turfing this one to me, huh?"

"If it helps, think of yourself as the outside expert."

"Right."

"So should I tell Dr. Lonigan you're good to go then?"

I'd done worse to pay the rent. From the information given, I didn't believe the theory about the owl; but the sightings of what looked like a falconer, if credible, sounded intriguing. Some kind of nut case maybe, one who'd gotten a little training in how to handle a raptor, a licensed rehabber or falconer or someone who had worked with one.

"Okay," I said. "I'll do it."

"Righteous . . . ." I could almost hear Darla beaming through the phone.

"But you'll need to throw in an extra set of plane tickets."

"What for?"

"For Nicky. She's a falconer herself and she may actually have a better feel for dealing with this type of situation than I do. It won't increase the fee."

Darla cleared her throat. "I'll check with Dr. Lonigan. I don't think that will be any problem. But I also need to warn you about a couple of other things. First, in addition to being a physician, Dr. Lonigan has been a longtime animal rights activist."

"Oookay . . . You might have sprung that little ditty on me sooner."

"I know, I know. But listen, the other thing she wants me to tell you . . . you're probably aware of the friction between some bird watchers and cat owners over cats running loose killing songbirds?"

"Some. I suppose."

"Well, a group of birdwatchers up here in the city read about the story and Dr. Lonigan's accusations in the paper. And they've apparently taken an interest in the matter, along with Lonigan's animal rights group. There has already been a small protest, some picketing and counter-picketing, that sort of thing."

Oh, boy. "No going to sea in a pea-green boat then either, I suppose."

"Huh?"

"Owl and the pussy cat," I said.

CPSIA information can be obtained at www.ICGtesting.com
Printed in the USA
LVOW06s1432170915

454593LV00001B/110/P

9 780989 146524